# ONE-SHOT

## JACY MORRIS

Published by Crystal Lake Publishing—Where Stories Come Alive!

Website: www.crystallakepub.com

# PRAISE

"Jacy Morris writes like he is punishing stasis. Like he has a bone to pick with the status quo…and why not? The status quo is boring as fuck and has always served to keep new, vital voices down. Voices like Jacy Morris'."

– Matt Blairstone, publisher/founder, Tenebrous Press

"Morris's writing is vivid, fast, and smooth as top-shelf whiskey. He's a must-read author for me. If you haven't tried his fiction yet, check out ONE-SHOT to see what you've been missing. Highly recommended!"

– Brian Bowyer, author of *Flesh Rehearsal*

"I just couldn't put this book down. One-Shot takes the "loser" character type and goes deep, exploring generational and cultural identity, accompanied by just the right touch of supernatural horror. Jacy Morris has a knack for witty humor and one-liners that land every time. He paints vivid scenes with just a couple of phrases, immersing you more than lengthy paragraphs could."

– Carlos E. Rivera, author of *The Local Truth* and *Blackout*

Torrid Waters is the pulp and extreme horror imprint of Crystal Lake. For this book, the author has supplied the following trigger warnings: abortion, infanticide, smoking, drinking, sex.

# Prologue

The woman below pulled him deeper inside.

*So, if I'm seven-sixteenths Native, then this kid'll be like…three-and-a-half sixteenths? And then, that kid's kids'll be…uhh.*

"Fuck me, One-Shot!"

He thrusted, closing his eyes to avoid seeing her face. She wasn't ugly, just not his type. He pictured a face—rounded, pale, with deep, anime-style eyes. That face had a name, but he didn't like to think it anymore; her name came with too much pain.

*Ah, fuck faces.*

In his mind's eye, the face disappeared, replaced by the body he'd coveted, so different from the soft, near-middle-aged lady below him. Breasts like softballs, rippling ribs, flesh the color of lilies.

He came.

Rolling over, he sat on the edge of the bed, his cock dangling downward, a drip of white fluid hanging from the tip—his gift, liquid and potent. Without it, he was nothing. Without it, his tribe was nothing. "It's done."

The woman ran a hand across his back, and gooseflesh broke out on his arms. "How can you know?" she asked.

One-Shot laughed. "I just know. Give it a week. We'll do a couple of tests. You'll see."

"I want more," the woman groaned. She was not unattractive. Many men might pay her to be in One-Shot's position, but he wasn't interested. This was purely a business transaction.

He stood and stepped into his jeans and underwear at the same time. His thirst grew. Stuffing his cock down in his briefs, he zipped his pants and tried not to look at the naked woman on the bed. "I got places to be."

"Another woman?"

One-Shot smiled. "That wouldn't be responsible. Safety…remember? Safety's my middle name."

"You can do anything you want," the woman enticed.

"What I want is a beer." He pulled his shirt on over his head and ran a hand through his hair. "Gimme a call in a week. We'll do the tests."

The woman on the bed pouted. They did that sometimes. But he wasn't being paid to show them a good time. He was being paid to put a baby inside them. Anything else would make him a whore. A man had to have standards, had to be able to look himself in the mirror, something One-Shot could do three times out of four, which wasn't half bad in his opinion.

"I'll see myself out," he said.

The sky hung dark and pregnant, the city roads slick with moisture. The humidity made it feel as if he walked through a living, breathing armpit. In his rearview mirror, he caught the crackling light of a thunderbolt as it arced to the ground. A moment later, the sky's water broke, thundering against the windshield of his car until it seemed like the entire world had become a car wash. The raindrops, fat and boisterous, pounded on the hood of his Honda Accord, made him think maybe they were going to leave dents. Even if they did, it wouldn't matter; his car was a piece of shit on wheels.

He parked on the street, pulled over to the side of Fifth Avenue, checked his mirrors to see if anyone was close enough to carjack him. Not that his vehicle was anything worth stealing, but you never knew. Around here, even an old junker like his was worth the price of a hotel room and a few hot meals. He could have afforded something better, could have taken out a payment, but that wasn't his way. He'd grown up poor, and goddamn it, he hadn't climbed out of the ranks of poverty by being frivolous with his money.

One-Shot was cheap when it came to luxury items like cars. Rather, he chose to splurge on the things that counted—booze, women, the NFL package.

Rain pelted his vehicle, and he worried it would force its way through the roof. Leaning on the center console, he pulled out his phone, scanned the messages, and waited for the rain to abate. Rain like this couldn't go on forever.

*"Where u at?"* Corey texted.

He brought up the keyboard, typed out a reply: *"Waiting 4 the rain to stop. There in a minute."*

As the rain machine-gunned his car, he checked his email for more clients. The toughest part about One-Shot's chosen profession was there was no repeat business. He was a one-and-done kind of guy, hence the nickname.

One-Shot wasn't his real name, but it was the name everyone called him, except for family, and the rare woman he got serious about. Hell, he doubted anyone in his inner circle even remembered his real name, which was fine by him. Arnold was such a fucked name, about two decades past its prime when his parents named him. But his mother had read a book by some Indian dude with a character named Arnold, so here he was. No, One-Shot was a better name than all that.

Without warning, a woman with brown skin and wearing a tight dress plopped into his car. One-Shot reached over and locked the driver's door in case she was part of a scam to get him not to pay attention while someone snuck up behind him and jacked his ass. He reached down into the pocket of the driver's side door, wrapping his hands around something cold and metal.

"Jesus fuck," the woman said.

She dripped, her purse soaking the bare carpet of his ride with rainwater.

"What the hell are you doing?" he asked, trying not to be angry with the woman. He understood. Any port in a storm and all that, but still, he had to hear her say it before he could relax. This part of Pittsburgh wasn't the worst part of town, but it wasn't necessarily the safest either.

"Relax. I'm just trying to keep dry. I just got douched out there."

At this, One-Shot laughed, let his fingers slide off the grip of his pistol. His eyes wandered over her legs, admiring them, the shape, the curve of her calf, the way the wet material of her skirt clung to her thighs. There was a time when One-Shot would have made a run at her, gone for her simply because he thought it was a sign from fate. But those days were gone.

Now, he simply felt sorry for the woman, for how she had gotten drenched by a storm out of the middle of nowhere.

Lightning crackled. It struck the ground a hundred yards behind his car. He waited for a fire to start, for flames to build, but nothing came, and he wondered if he had actually seen a lightning bolt or just imagined it. Onward the rain marched, falling in sheets, the streetlights of Fifth Avenue transformed into stars through the veil of water cascading down his windshield.

"I'm Kennedy." She held out her hand. Her palm was soft and warm, and he shook it, smiling.

He could tell her his real name, could say it here underwater, whisper it once. It would stay here, never to be shared or uttered again. Things behind the waterfall were secret, always were, in movies and video games. Once, when he was a kid, his grandfather had taken him to a nature park, complete with a waterfall. He'd swum behind it, only to find more rocks, hard, with nary a treasure chest in sight. He'd been lied to his whole life, so he continued the tradition.

"Name's One-Shot."

The woman laughed, her teeth white and large in the artificial starlight. "What are you, some sort of gangster?"

One-Shot smiled. He laughed along with Kennedy, showing her he wasn't offended. He knew how ridiculous the name was, knew it drove a wedge between him and other people. That wedge protected him, kept him from getting hurt. He didn't want the pain—the people who went for a man named One-Shot were incapable of hurting him. Damaged and broken themselves, they couldn't be loved, wouldn't allow themselves to experience the greatest and worst of all human emotions. One-Shot kept them at arm's length. "I impregnate women for money."

The smile fell from Kennedy's face. "So you're a prostitute?"

One-Shot continued to smile. "Not quite." Kennedy was handling this better than he had expected.

The rain slacked off, and the last trickles worked their way down the windshield. Kennedy looked out at the rivers in the gutters. He could tell she didn't want to go, didn't want to step into the sodden world, but he had places to be.

"That's our sign," One-Shot said. He turned the engine off and unlocked his door. "I'm heading up to the pizza place on the corner. You wanna hit it up with me?"

Kennedy turned to him and smiled. "Do I look like I eat pizza?"

One-Shot sneered. She didn't. "I'm not going there for the pizza. I'm going there for the booze."

"You asking me out on a date?"

"Not a date." He paused then, gave her heart time to beat. "Just one shot. We'll see where it goes from there."

She laughed a bit, the type of laugh that told him he wasn't all that clever, but he was clever enough. "Alright."

They stepped from the car. One-Shot soaked his foot up to the ankle in the gutter, chilling it to the bone instantly. When he stepped on the sidewalk, his sock squished in his shoe. He hated being wet, especially cold and wet. He opened the back passenger door, reached into the pouch on the rear of the driver's seat, and pulled out an umbrella.

Walking around the car, he popped the umbrella open and handed it to Kennedy. With the press of his fob, he locked his car, and they journeyed down the sidewalk until they came to an ugly business—a pizza place on Fifth Avenue, directly behind the arena where the Penguins played. He liked hockey, wished it was still hockey season. He loved to go to a game by himself, sit among the crowd, and soak in the sounds and sights, a tallboy of I.C. Light in his hands. But it was early summer now, so no hockey for him.

The front of Pizza Italia looked like the entrance to a Christian bookstore, bland and lacking personality. The pizza sold inside was the same. But on the west side of the building, there was something better than pizza—a bar, dark and populated by blue-collar folk. He recognized a lot of the faces and knew most of their names. Walk into this place on any given weekday night, and you'd find the same folk bellied up to the bar.

The woman behind the bar whirled, mixing drinks and pouring shots with the greatest of ease. One-Shot appreciated her speed. Quite often, in a bar where everyone knew each other, bartenders tended to spend more time talking than making cocktails. But Desby could do both at the same time. Her frazzled blonde hair wreathed her head, overprocessed and frizzy. Pale arms stuck out of a white tank top, a tattoo of crackling lightning running down the left one.

With a gentle hand on Kennedy's shoulder, he guided her to the bar. In the middle of one of her patented mixing and pouring whirls, Desby said, "What'll it be, One-Shot?"

"Let's make it two tonight," he said, nodding at the girl to his right. Desby gave him a wink and spun away, always moving.

"Hey! There he is. My man."

One-Shot turned and greeted the man with a half hug. Corey had been a good friend for a long time—never judged, never fought. He was good times with a heartbeat, and One-Shot always knew where to find him. When he wanted to put his head on hold, Corey was his guy.

"Good to see you, man."

"And who is this?" Corey asked, his eyes going wide.

"Kennedy, this is Corey. Corey, Kennedy."

"And what's a woman like you doing with a piece of shit like this?" Corey asked.

One-Shot didn't care. He hadn't brought Kennedy in here for himself. Wasn't interested in her at all. He hadn't been interested in anyone since the woman whose name he didn't like to think.

"He saved me from the rain, offered to buy me a drink."

As soon as she said the words, Desby appeared, two shots of whiskey, nothing fancy. Desby knew his tastes, knew he didn't like splurging on expensive shit when the cheap shit got the job done.

One-Shot slid one of the shot glasses to Kennedy, picked up his own, and said, "Here's to new friends."

They knocked them back, and when Kennedy placed her glass back on the counter, One-Shot caught Corey's eye and nodded his head at Kennedy. Corey nodded back.

His friend circled behind them, stood at Kennedy's right elbow, leaning on the bar and continuing the conversation with Kennedy stuck in the middle. It was a simple tactic, but handy when you wanted to foist a woman off on your friend. As the night wore on and Desby continued pouring drinks, Kennedy fell for Corey. Corey could do that. It was easy for him. He was a good guy.

Around eleven, with Corey leaning in close to Kennedy, and Kennedy leaning right back, One-Shot's cell phone buzzed. His hopes of another client were dashed when he saw the name on the phone. *Sister.* He replayed the word in his head, saying it like Darth Vader at the end of *The Empire Strikes Back*, in the dulcet tones of James Earl Jones.

*Fuck.*

He stepped from the bar, wandered a little way into the dark booths where only tourists sat. The worn vinyl seat squeaked as he plopped down, quickly yanking his hand from the sticky surface. Desby might kick ass behind the bar, but when it came to cleaning the rest of the place, she wasn't so hot. He supposed that was why she worked in this dump despite her obvious talents. That and the fact she drank as many shots as she poured. Many were the nights when One-Shot had driven Desby home. She was broken and sad in some ways, and that suited One-Shot just fine.

*We all have our things.*

With his head swimming, One-Shot looked down at his phone. Read the message with bleary eyes. His sister's words made him panic. *"Give me a call. Urgent."*

# Chapter 1: On the Road – Day One

*Now*

The road to the west started out cool. There were all these little islands of gas stations and fast-food joints, and the lights of the cities slid by like watching a movie. You saw signs for places you've never heard of like Twinsburg, Macedonia, and Vermilion. Your imagination went wild trying to explain the origin of these town names. Like, what fucking twins was the town of Twinsburg named after? In his head, he imagined some sort of *Village of the Damned* kids running around, at least five of them. Maybe one of them was dead and buried, or maybe they ate a sixth one in the womb, chomped it right up, and that's how they got their superpowers. He imagined Twinsburg consisted of one creepy house with a post office address. You could stop there if you wanted to, but you'd never get out. It was that type of place, One-Shot supposed.

As his beer buzz wore off and his stomach began to grumble, he attuned to the timeless drone of the road. In a car, given a bottomless tank of gasoline, one could outrun anything. They could outrun their flaws, their bills, their job, the fucking shame of re-opening the wounds of an ex-fiancée. Most of all, they could outrun their mistakes, only seeing them when they glanced into the rearview mirror. Then you might find them sitting back there, blood leaking from their eyes, teeth broken and busted, the hair on their heads matted with death. But hey, even your mistakes liked the road. On the road, you could focus on the eternal yellow lines and forget about the specters you dragged along in the backseat.

As the morning brightened, One-Shot's adrenaline wore off, and it wasn't long before he needed to buy gas. The first place he stopped was one of those fancy truck stops, lines of semi-trucks pulled over in a huge parking lot, a country-style diner attached to the convenience store. Inside, he bought everything he thought he'd need for the trip: some medicine, Marlboro Reds, a couple of Red Bulls, a twelve pack of Dr. Pepper, a bag of peppered beef jerky, and some Peanut M&Ms.

Refusing to put down Grandpa for even one second—he wasn't going to be able to go back home if he got Grandpa stolen—he carried all his purchases to the cash register one by one. The exhausted cashier stared at him like he might be a meth-head. When he was ready, he paid and asked for a bag.

The cashier took his time about it, a sneer on his face. "Whatchu got in the urn?" the man asked. "You got some gak in there?"

"Just my grandpa."

"Uh-huh," the cashier said, clearly not believing him.

Maybe it was One-Shot's fault. He probably should have used something besides duct tape to seal the top of the urn. Duct tape made it look like some jury-rigged solution. No wonder the cashier thought it was full of meth.

Before he got in the car, he opened the passenger-side door and buckled in Grandpa.

*Thanks.*

"No problem, Grandpa."

An old women looked at him like he was nuts, but he didn't give a shit. Who gives a fuck what you do at a gas station? No one remembers a gas station person. Everyone at a gas station might as well be walking around in ski masks. That's how unimportant people are in those settings.

With Grandpa strapped in, he ran around the car, keeping his eye on the shine of the brass urn in the morning light, lest some shady fuck came along and plucked it out of the vehicle when he wasn't looking.

Once inside, he packed the smokes, slapping them on his wrist five times, ripping the cellophane off, then the interior foil. He set the open pack in his console, along with a multicolored lighter with the word "Pisces" on the side. In gaudy blues and whites, two fish encircled each other on the lighter. If he stared at it long enough, it looked like the fins on their bodies moved, like they would pop right off the lighter and go swimming around in the interior of his car.

One-Shot shook his head, realized he was getting tired, and then dug into the plastic bag. He came out with a silver and blue can, popped the top, took a healthy slug, and choked down the sour-sweet liquid. It burned the back of his throat, and with the liquid energy coursing through his veins, he started the engine, floored it out of the no-name truck stop, and merged onto the highway.

He flew along I-80, riding a mammoth wave of cars all heading somewhere and nowhere at the same time, a school of metallic fish shoaling at seventy-miles-per-hour.

Grandpa wasn't a fun passenger. *It's all the same, Palmer. It's all the same. Everyone's doing the same thing. Everyone's unhappy, everyone thinks they're owed more. Make the most of it while you got it, my dear, my dear, my reindeer.*

"Ain't that the truth." He missed the night. As the sun rose, busting through the rear windshield to live in his rearview mirror, all he saw were rundown homes and fast-food restaurants built taller than they needed to be. Their signs jutted into the air like penises, ready to fuck anyone who dared become hungry while driving down the highway. There were also office buildings, plain and utilitarian, and a thousand cars all spilling exhaust into the morning air.

Along with the sun came the heat. Near the end of July, the middle of the country baked, with the foliage sweating as bad as the people, turning the air into a molten miasma. As he drove, his only company was the sound of cars rushing by, the wind from his rolled down window, and the constant snapping and flapping of his garbage bag window.

One-Shot looked longingly at the empty hole in his console where the radio had been. What kind of asshole broke into a car to steal the radio? The lowest of lowlifes, the type of motherfucker who'd bang your girl and then send you a photo of it. He hoped whoever had stolen his stereo had dropped it and broken their foot, or at least scraped a knuckle or two getting the damn thing out.

*Sing me a song.*

"I don't know any songs," One-Shot said.

*You know songs. No one will know.*

One-Shot cleared his throat, reached into the console for a smoke. He closed the window long enough to light up, then he cracked the window to create a vacuum to suck all the smoke out. As he puffed and smoke swirled around the interior of his vehicle, he ran through his mental jukebox. His family had always been musical. Seldom were the times when music wasn't playing. He'd gotten out of the habit when he'd moved in with Sadie. She came from a quiet family, and she couldn't have any noise at night or she'd wake up.

Lying in bed next to Sadie, he would toss and turn for her sake. During these times, the world ran through his mind, a nonstop river of worries, plans, makeshift schemes to get out of the nine-to-five life, plans that would never see fruition. Eventually, faced with the prospect of exhaustion, he would pick out a song he knew from his youth, sing it repeatedly in his head. That usually knocked him right out.

Right then, his mind was drawing a blank though. By the time he'd burned through his cigarette and tossed it out the window, he'd come up empty.

*Try The Stanley Brothers.*

"I don't know any of those songs."

Grandpa remained silent, and One-Shot could hear the disappointment in the stillness.

Amid the snapping of the garbage bag, and the howl of air through the still-cracked window, a snatch of something came to him, as if borne on the wind. Maybe it was the field of waving grass on the side of the road that brought the memory back, conjured the song as if out of thin air. Bluegrass.

He opened his mouth, let a nasally snatch of lyrics come out. He sang a Stanley Brother's tune, out of pitch, haunting and warbly the way they had played it. The song was about a man who went back to his hometown and found nothing but strangers. No one who knew his face or name.

The miles rolled on and the dotted white lines disappeared, the cars vanishing along with them. All that was left was his voice, backed by the howling air rushing through his car, and the silent somberness of Grandpa. He liked the old man better when he was alive.

***A few days ago***

"He's dead," said his sister.

"Oh."

"Is that all you have to say?"

It was all he *could* say. "Oh," he repeated. "Oh." Pain lanced through his body, a cocktail stronger than anything Desby could have mixed up. A homeless man walked by, and One-Shot must have looked pretty bad right then, because the poor, piss-smelling dude didn't even bug him for spare change.

Raven talked a little more, said the words *heart attack*, but that's all One-Shot heard. "You okay?" She always did that, asked him what he was feeling. Grandpa had always joked that One-Shot had gotten the brains while Raven had gotten all the emotions.

"Yeah," he muttered. The world spun around him, not because of the alcohol; he was used to that.

Silence.

He didn't know what to say, never knew what to do when people died. Death was a hard thing; expected or unexpected, it didn't matter.

"Come home, Arnold," Raven said.

"Yeah."

"I love you."

One-Shot sighed and said, "Love you, too."

Raven hung up, and One-Shot stood trying to figure out the next step. He should have been a better brother, should have asked Raven how she was doing. But that was hard to do when he didn't even know how he was doing. *How do I feel?*

*I feel nothing.*

*I'm bad.*

*I should feel something.*

*Maybe I do…and I just don't know it.*

One-Shot headed back into Pizza Italia. He needed another drink.

In a daze, he walked up to the bar.

Corey must have sensed he was off. "You okay, man?"

"Yeah."

"You don't look okay."

"My grandpa died."

The smile fell from Corey's face, and he moved around Kennedy. She was Corey's now, but he could sense the sympathy in her eyes. Didn't want it. Corey placed a hand on his shoulder. A lump formed in One-Shot's throat.

Desby whirled over, took one look at him, and asked. "What's going on?"

One-Shot couldn't speak. He'd used up all his words.

"His grandpa just died," Corey said.

Desby's face broke with sympathy, and it made the lump in One-Shot's throat swell. He didn't think he could breathe if it got any bigger.

Desby whirled away, and like a paramedic delivering a dose of Narcan to an overdosing junkie, she slid a shot across the bar. "Here you go. On the house."

One-Shot nodded, reached out with a shaking hand, and gripped the shot glass. He held it there, his head down, the entire world pressing down upon him.

The rest of the night blurred together.

In the morning, he awakened in Desby's bed. She snored, ripping the air apart with her dry throat. He sat up, and his brain tried to escape his skull.

His clothes lay crumpled on the floor. He pulled his jeans off the dingy carpet and fished around in the pocket for his phone.

Raven's words: "Where are you?"

He leaned back on the bed, resting on one of Desby's thighs.

After a ceremonial wiping of his hands across his face, he stood. He had things to do.

He left without saying goodbye. He'd done it before. Desby didn't care, or if she did, she kept the secret in her chest.

Outside, the city baked in the noontime air, the heat rising, the humidity not helping his hangover. Onward he trudged, checking his pocket three times to see if he still had his keys on him, as if they could disappear at any moment. In a daze, he slogged down the city streets, heading back to where he thought he left his car.

Last night felt like a bad dream. At one point, he stopped, pulled his phone from his pocket, and re-read Raven's message again to make sure he hadn't dreamed it. *"Call me. Urgent."*

*Grandpa's dead. He's really gone.*

"I'm such a piece of shit," he muttered to himself, drawing side-eye from a woman on her lunch break, a cup of coffee in her hand.

His relationship with his grandfather had been a special thing, and like most special things, it had its up and downs. His grandfather had practically raised him.

It's not like his parents were dead or anything. They simply had their own issues to deal with. When he was ten, One-Shot's father had disappeared, and his mother had chased after him, leaving her two kids in Pittsburgh. His father was an Appalachian man, not made for the city. He was also an alcoholic who couldn't hold a steady job or keep it in his pants. His mother wasn't much better.

So Grandpa had stepped up. He'd been an FBI agent before he retired and settled down in Pittsburgh. One-Shot remembered spending long Pittsburgh evenings on the porch of his grandfather's American foursquare house, listening to the Pirates play on the radio while his grandfather sipped coffee and smoked cigarettes.

It wasn't an ideal childhood due to the abandonment, but it had been better than what most people had experienced. He had been taken care of and loved, but there was always the feeling within that he hadn't been good enough. That he hadn't been special enough for his parents to want to stick around and be a part of his life.

Oh, they called on his birthday, sent him gifts at Christmas. And whenever he went to West Virginia to visit, they made a big deal about it, took him around the places they frequented in the small town where they lived. For a day or two, he would think, *This is good. I could live here.* Then, three days into his visit, they would drink—get "three sheets" they called it—and sit around the kitchen table sobbing and apologizing and telling him how proud of him they were. Then, they'd get four sheets, and they'd start getting mean, accusing him of not being a good son, telling him he needed to call more often. His mother would tell him he needed to find a nice Indian girl to marry, and his father would ask him when he was going to have kids.

In these times, under the sail of four sheets, they would reveal themselves as who they were and what they thought. That's about the time he would leave, hop in his car, and drive from West Virginia to Pittsburgh and hole up at his grandfather's house for a few days. His grandfather didn't mind. He liked to have the company. They could sit and talk for hours, play chess, watch a ballgame on TV. They never talked about anything important, but sometimes that was better than hashing out your feelings.

Now Grandpa was gone, and with him, he had taken a part of One-Shot—the part Grandpa still referred to as Palmer—plucked it right from One-Shot's chest and carried it to his grave with him.

*Wait…is he being buried? Is he being cremated?*

One-Shot's face turned red. *I should know this. What kind of grandson am I?* Though he felt like laying on the ground and curling into a ball, he pressed onward, waiting at the interminably long crossing lights on Fifth Avenue, fighting the urge to puke up the evening's pleasure.

By the time he made it to the car, a sheen of alcohol-infused sweat layered his body. When he got to his vehicle, he sighed. The back window had been busted out. Bits of glass lay on the sidewalk like discarded dreams. He opened the door and peered inside. The stereo was gone. In a panic, he opened the driver's side door and checked for his handgun. A small glint of silver flashed in his eyes, and he leaned on the edge of the open car door. At least one thing had gone right.

Swiping the sweat off his brow, he hopped in his car. Hot air blasted through the broken window, drowning out any of the cooling his car's struggling air conditioner could have provided. At home, he took a shower, drank a beer to get right, and then pulled a garbage bag and a roll of duct tape from under the sink. The entire time, his phone buzzed with messages from his mom and sister. One-Shot doubted his dad would have left West Virginia, even for a death. Some people were just meant to stay home their entire lives. But not One-Shot.

With his broken window sealed by a black garbage bag, he drove across town to his grandfather's house with the makeshift window snapping and billowing like a sail. He parked against the curb about a block down and fought the urge to drive off into oblivion, somewhere far away, like California. Probably lots of people there could use his services—maybe movie stars who were too busy with their careers to find proper love.

He reached into the compartment of his car's console and pulled out a pack of smokes. His nerves were shot, he felt like shit, and he had no idea what he would be walking into inside Grandpa's house. In his ideal version of the future, everyone would be appropriately somber, heads down, but respectful. They would sit around the kitchen table and slurp coffee like Grandpa. Hell, they might even pour out a cup for him, see if his spirit would come and take a sip. Then, they would cry and hug. Next, they would get down to the business of death—what to do about the body, who to invite to the funeral…if there was even going to be a funeral. Honestly, Grandpa had known no one, kept to himself more than most people his age. The only people he had time for was family.

*I should have visited more often.*

He lit the cigarette and took a deep drag, letting the smoke fill his lungs. He liked to think this one counted as ceremonial use, as if he was cleansing himself before walking into his grandfather's house. One-Shot laughed at his own maudlin thoughts. He wasn't spiritual in the least. Smoke was just smoke, the combusted particles of something else, light and feathery, floating due to heat differential between the smoke and the air.

The real reason he smoked was because it was medicinal, because he knew there was something wrong with him and only cigarettes could help. There was something wrong with his whole family. He couldn't put his finger on it, couldn't explain it in words, but there was something wrong with every one of them, except for Grandpa… Well, maybe less so than the rest of them.

One-Shot knew his idealized version of what would happen when he walked into Grandpa's house was nothing more than a peace-pipe dream. In reality, he'd walk in, find his sister in teary-eyed shambles and his mother working on upping her sheet count. This early in the day, she might just be at one, but hard at work on sheet number two. He would stand there, empty, dreading what was to come, every negative feeling heading his way, and he would shut down. It's what he did. It was what he'd done when his parents had gone away. It's what he'd done when his ex had…done what she'd done.

He blew smoke into the air, lifted his hand to the keys still hanging from the ignition. He turned them--not far enough to start the car, but far enough to turn the electrics on. He tossed his half-smoked medication onto the street, rolled the window up, and then turned the car off. With his keys in hand, he stuffed them in his jeans and stepped out of the car into the too bright day.

The street had barely changed since he had first come to the neighborhood, immediately moving into a large, empty square room on the second floor of Grandpa's house. As a child, he'd slept on wooden floors without a scrap of furniture. For the first year, he'd slept on a blue-green roll of soft foam shaped like the inside of an eggshell carton. He missed those days, still slept on the floor every now and then as a way to reclaim his past. Because even though those times hung bloody with trauma, there was something in those memories that felt like home.

He climbed the brick steps leading to the wraparound porch. From the corner of his eye, he could see the table where

Grandpa used to chill. The black circle of the plastic ashtray sat on the pollen-stained glass. One-Shot didn't want to look directly at it, just wanted to pretend Grandpa was still sitting over there, smoking and sipping on his coffee. If he looked over there and didn't see him, he would be forced to digest the truth.

When he started feeling like a freak, he shook his head and walked inside. He put away One-Shot and became Arnold once more.

He didn't know what he had expected to find in Grandpa's house, but this was not it.

Raven stood in the kitchen frying up egg sandwiches. His mom sat at the table, her head in her hands, her eyes red-rimmed with sorrow.

When the screen door slammed shut behind him, his mother lifted her head and rose from the kitchen table with her arms held in the air like a zombie. She swooped in for the kill, which turned out to be just a hug. He returned it, not letting the comfort of motherly contact settle too deep in his chest. *It's only a matter of time.*

After what seemed like an interminably long while, she let go. Her eyes were dark circles, and for the first time, he realized her veil of immortality had slipped. She was getting up there, into that age bracket when Death comes knocking at the door like a Jehovah's Witness, undeterred by someone not answering, waiting with the patience of an oak tree.

"Come. Sit down. Raven's making some breakfast."

It was one in the afternoon, but in his family that still meant breakfast. No one in their family got up before noon if given a choice. Was it a family trait or a Native American trait?

He couldn't tell you. The only people he'd personally lived with who had gotten up early were his dad, who believed fish ate in the morning, and her...the name he didn't want to say.

"So, how's Sadie, Arnold?"

*She said it.*

Raven tried to catch her mom's eye and shake her head, but Mom was clueless. Oh, Three Sheets Mom might have caught the look. Three Sheets Mom was hyper-sensitive, saw slights where there were none, could tell when you lied, knew if you were thinking about doing something you shouldn't. But this Mom—this terrible, droopy-eyed, grieving thing—wasn't picking up on much.

"I don't know," One-Shot said.

His mother sighed, leaned back in her chair. "I'd always hoped you'd get back together."

*No, you didn't. You were disappointed she was white. Couldn't have been clearer about it, in fact. You lie. Only now that the problem is out of your hair, you pretend like you liked her.* "It's not in the cards, I guess."

Mom nodded, and the conversation went dead. Arnold didn't know what to do or what to say. One night, one text, one phone call, that's all it had taken to change his world. It had happened before...with Sadie. Hell, he ought to be getting used to it by now, his life changing in the blink of an eye.

"Are you seeing anyone else?"

Arnold shook his head.

His mother nodded.

Thank Christ for Raven. She used a greasy spatula to place an egg sandwich on a plate, and then, with three plates balanced on her arms, she brought them to the table. Raven, despite being the one with the emotions, seemed to be the only person acting like her normal self. She smiled at him, and he felt like a bad brother. He couldn't remember the last time he'd called her, asked her how she was doing, and yet, here she was making him a fucking sandwich. There's nothing quite like looking into the face of a taken-for-granted loved one to see all your own insecurities reflected back at you.

He wondered what his mother saw when she looked at his face. What did Raven see? He hoped they saw only the good things he felt about them. The bad things were his burden to carry. Let them be happy with who they are, even if they couldn't be happy about who he was.

His last conversation with Raven ended with her storming out of Chachi's Sports Pub. He shouldn't have told her about his career, about…being One-Shot. But when he'd offered to pay for her drinks and her meal, she had gotten suspicious, started accusing him of being a drug dealer.

"Gimme some, Arnold. Word on the street is you got the hookup. You better give me some before they put your ass in jail," she'd teased. "So what is it? Weed, pills, coke?"

He sort of wished it had been any of those three things. Raven would have reacted better if he *had* been a drug dealer.

"You're giving people Indian babies?" she'd scoffed.

"I know what you're thinking," he tried to explain.

"You're disgusting."

"It's not like that."

"You're sick, Arnie. Just plowing your way through women for money. You're a whore."

"They just want children," he said.

"So, they should go out on a fucking date! You don't buy a little Indian baby. That's messed up."

"Most of these ladies are too busy working, and they're not getting any younger. If it wasn't for me, they might never have children."

"Maybe that's the point. If they can't make time to find a father for their child, then maybe they shouldn't be having one in the first place."

Arnold had to admit, he'd had the same thought a few times. "Don't judge them," he said. "Don't judge me."

"Too late," Raven said. Then she drained her beer, flipped him off, and stormed out.

It had taken him a while to understand her reaction to his new vocation, but in the end, he figured it had something to do with Raven not knowing her actual dad. She and Arnold had different fathers. He knew his—kind of wished he didn't—but Raven only knew her father by his name.

Maybe, in her mind, what he was doing was the same as what her father had done to Mom—knocked her up and then disappeared. It was the paradox of his mother. Though she wanted him to keep it in the tribe, her own experience with a Native American man had been nothing short of disastrous. Oh, she got his sister out of it, but little else. But Raven was alright, could make a mean egg sandwich as well.

He bit into the sandwich, relishing the grease, the salt, the pepper, the melted tang of a slice of American cheese.

"Where is Grandpa?" Arnold finally asked.

"He's at the funeral home. They're taking care of him," his mom said, tears brimming in her eyes.

"We gonna do a funeral?"

Raven spoke up then, which made sense. She was the only one good with money, with putting things in order, jumping through the hundreds of hoops the world made you leap through at any given moment. If there was an Olympics for figuring out how to do something, Raven would have won the gold medal. He pictured her in a gymnast's outfit, running from one desk to another, filling out forms with reckless abandon, initializing here, here, and here, and then carrying her papers over to another desk to have them notarized. Then it was off to the post office before they closed to get the papers out in the mail. Yeah, she'd be good at that.

As for himself, he could barely remember to pay his bills on time. Sometimes he forgot to do it until something in his apartment didn't work anymore, like the water, electricity, whatever. Raven always claimed he was fucking up his credit, that he'd want it one day. But credit was bullshit, the white man's dream, to have imaginary money based upon the simple fact that you could possibly pay it off at some point. Credit was for suckers as far as Arnold could tell. If you didn't have the money to buy something, then for God's sake, don't fucking buy it.

"Grandpa wanted to be cremated," Raven said.

For some reason, this bothered him. It meant he wouldn't be able to see his grandpa's body. The next time he saw him, he'd be a pile of ashes in an urn. Arnold didn't want him cremated. He wanted him buried in the ground, so he could get drunk every now and then and go and sit at his grave, his grandfather reclining six-feet-deep in his coffin, magically hearing every word he said through one-hundred-cubic-feet of dirt, worms, and grass. Maybe they could put a little pipe running from his coffin to the surface, and they could blow smoke down there and drip coffee to him. Grandpa'd like that.

It was different talking to an urn. Or so he imagined. He'd never actually had a family member he cared about die before. His grandmother, Grandpa's wife, had passed away when he was young. Heart attack, they said.

His uncle, who he only remembered as a rounded face with brown skin, had passed away when he was five. All he remembered about him was that he smelled like cigarettes and cologne, and his mother had cried for weeks. No one ever really spoke about Uncle Harry's death, though, over the years, he'd gathered it was suicide.

"Why cremated?" he asked.

Raven shrugged, and his mother looked away. Arnold got the feeling she was hiding something, but he didn't feel like drawing it out of her. Didn't know how to even go about it. They ate their sandwiches in silence.

When they finished, Arnold stood up and stepped outside. Family made him feel…uncomfortable, as if he was playing with fire while wearing a gasoline-soaked sweater. At any moment, he expected his sister to yell at him for being irresponsible. If Raven didn't start in on him, then it was only a matter of time before his mother started pressuring him into giving her Indian grandkids. He didn't know why she wanted them so bad; she would make a shit grandmother.

For as good as Grandpa had been at being a grandfather, Arnold couldn't imagine ever letting a kid of his stay with Mom and Dad. No thanks. What a nightmare that would be. They'd get four sheets and wind up leaving the poor kid playing in the fucking oven or some shit.

On the front porch, the sun had the audacity to shine bright and true. Small clouds drifted across the sky, unable to block the warming glory of the sun's rays. He slid his hand down into his pocket for his medicine. It was either that or he'd start walking toward his car and possibly never come back. *Why am I so bad at these things?*

As soon as he lit up, Raven stepped out onto the porch.

"I thought you quit," she said.

"Yeah, well, I didn't. I just told you that so you wouldn't worry."

"You're not going to run away, are you?"

"Psshh." He let the sound escape like the air from a punctured tire, the tires on his escape vehicle. Raven was good at that, calling him out on his bullshit. It was like she could read minds. With his tires slashed by her simple question, there was no chance he was going anywhere. He took a deep drag. "If you keep buggin' me, I am."

Raven leaned against the railing. She was getting older now too. Soon she'd start pumping out kids with that boyfriend of hers. He was no good in Arnold's book, a real piece of shit. "Where's your man?"

She got quiet then, looked away from him, and he knew he'd touched a nerve. He always did that, didn't seem to be able to have a conversation with his family without setting someone off. The only person he'd never had that problem with had been Grandpa.

"We're not together."

"Oh. I'm sorry." *Is that good enough? Is that enough? Goddamn it. Fuck this.* Around others, he was the picture of cool. Girls threw themselves at him. Guys wanted to be his friend. But put him next to someone who shared the same blood and all his powers went away. *'Oh, I'm sorry?' What the fuck kind of apology was that?*

They lapsed into silence, and Arnold put the cigarette to his lips once more, impatient for the time when he could be One-Shot again. As he pulled the cigarette from his lips and blew smoke into the air, Raven held out her hand.

"You don't smoke."

"It's ceremonial," she said.

"Get the fuck out of here."

"Maybe later."

"It's a nasty habit," he said.

"I know."

He smiled then. Raven was so easy to read. "How long have you been smoking?"

"Since I found out Marcus cheated on me."

He didn't have an answer for that. Filled with the guilt of being unable to make things better for his sister, he passed the cigarette her way, watched her take a drag with the greatest of familiarity. "You're full of shit. How long have you really been smoking?"

"I'll never tell," she said as she blew the smoke into the air. They smiled for a second, like they had in the old days, when they had been two kids abandoned by their parents, living in a strange part of Pittsburgh. They shared the smile the way they shared the cigarette, and then the memory of why they were here in the first place came back. It made them feel guilty for having not been miserable for a second. Their smiles faded, and they remembered their grandfather in their own way.

Arnold looked over his shoulder, made sure their mother wasn't standing at the window. "How long until she starts drinking?"

"I don't know," Raven said. "But if she doesn't start, I will."

Arnold knew what she meant. Their mother was in a bad place. Her hair was unkempt, and her eyes were baggy and ringed with dark circles from crying. She wasn't herself, and while she could be an unholy terror while drinking, he didn't relish the sight of her this forlorn. It pained him, and he didn't like pain.

"I'll race you to the fridge," he said. He flicked the cigarette into the rocky pea gravel, where it would burn itself down to the butt.

The two siblings pushed inside, their mouths watering for something that would taste better than the bitter grief and cigarette smoke residue currently occupying their mouths.

"Who was it?" their mother called from the living room. "I smelled the smoke in here!"

Neither of them answered as the siblings jostled each other in front of the fridge.

## *On the road*

He finished the song, his lungs unburdened from the pain of his past.

*Again,* Grandpa said.

One-Shot sang the song once more, disappearing into a trance. The hours rolled by, the states as well. He howled the lone Stanley Brothers tune he knew through Illinois and into Iowa until his voice grew raw. Ahead of him, the sun set, bathing his eyes in newborn orange light. As the light faded, dimming and purpling like a bruise, the song faded from his lips with it, and the road returned with its lines and its traffic.

His trance broke as the curve of the Earth ate the sun ahead of him. He found himself speeding along the highway at night, the road thin of vehicles, but for those who sped by at suicide speeds. One-Shot let them go, knew his vehicle couldn't keep up with one of those comets even had he wanted to. No, he was fine cruising along at his current speed, plodding across the United States. The tortoise, the hare, all that bullshit.

Most people, upon seeing the dark of the night, the emptiness of the highway, would have pulled over, found someplace to sleep off the rest of the evening. But not One-Shot. As the road stretched out before him, he began to see the entire ordeal as a challenge. He could do it all in one go, one shot, if you will. *Wouldn't that be a story to tell?*

*It certainly would be,* Grandpa said.

"Damn right."

There wasn't much to see in Iowa, not past the eastern border at least. The towns out here were far apart or hidden by row after row of corn. Occasionally, a truck stop would loom out of the night, appearing first as a speck of brightness, and then increasing in size until it almost seemed like it was daylight outside. Once he passed the truck stop, the process would continue in reverse. He began to feel like a space traveler, rocketing past sun after sun, one at a time, watching as they swelled in size and then diminished. Two light years away, Siletz waited.

*Don't go there,* Grandpa said.

One-Shot had trouble telling if Grandpa's words were in his head now, or merely the memory of something Grandpa had once told him around the kitchen table.

His spaceship, traveling at such high speeds, managed to take him back in time, pulling him out of his cockpit. The black road melted away, replaced by white cabinets in a too-bright dining room. His mouth opened to scream as his skin was pressed against his skull by some force. Centrifugal? Centripetal? Centipedal? They were all the same in time travel.

Instead of a scream, The Stanley Brothers' *Rank Stranger* issued forth from his throat.

From the corner of his eye, Grandpa pushed the lid off the urn, turned into a cloud that smelled faintly of Olympia Beer. The left headlight beam, a pool of light illuminating perhaps the next forty feet of road, transformed into the kitchen table. The right headlight beam transformed into a young One-Shot. But to Grandpa, he was just Palmer, his grandfather morphing his name from Arnold, to Arnold Palmer, and then finally, just the last name of a golfer One-Shot knew nothing about.

"Where are the other Indians?" Palmer asked. "How come it's just us?"

Grandpa shuffled a deck of Bicycle cards. The cards whooshed as they flexed into a flat deck once more, and Grandpa began "lining up his soldiers" as he called it. He sighed, and his lower teeth, packed in tight like the unmarked gravestones of a pauper's cemetery, stuck out as he composed his thoughts. "They got rid of 'em all."

"What do you mean?"

"The white man wanted it, so he pushed everyone out, sent 'em west, chased 'em, killed 'em, or made 'em march. But that didn't happen to us, to our tribe."

"What happened to our tribe?"

"You really want to know?"

Palmer nodded.

"Our tribes were small, perfectly sized for the areas we lived in. We were river people. We hunted some, gathered some more, but mostly, we spent our days fishing. The salmon would come jumping up the river as if they wanted to be eaten. You'd reach out with a net, scoop a couple up, and your day was done. Nothing but sunshine and naps after that.

"The white man saw this, said, 'That's not right.' So they took all our people, and a bunch of other tribes, dragged us off to a place called Siletz. It wasn't so bad. Small, but not so bad."

Palmer nodded, took in words that were maybe true, maybe made sense, but then again, maybe didn't until he was older. You could never be sure with time travel.

"Where is Siletz?" Palmer asked.

"In Oregon."

"Why aren't we there?"

His grandpa sighed, flipped through the cards in his hand to see if there was a play he could make. Having failed once more, he wiped the deck, reached into his shirt pocket to pull out an unfiltered Pall Mall.

"We're not there, because we don't belong there." He blew smoke through his mouth, and it hung between them.

"Why don't we belong?"

Grandpa rested the cigarette in an ashtray the color of maple syrup, a hazy streamer of smoke curling upward. The Stanley Brothers echoed in the background coming from a long way off. "Why do you ask so many questions?"

Palmer didn't. Never had, and that's how he knew Grandpa was hiding something.

"Forget about them. They want us there too much." He was frustrated now, his shuffling less precise. He reached out to his glass mug, thick and chunky, little concave circles shining in the sunlight.

"Palmer, Palmer, Palmer." He repeated the words like a mantra as he lined up his soldiers. "I want you to promise me you'll never go there."

Palmer remained quiet, and Grandpa lifted his head from his cards, stared at him from behind thick eyeglasses. "Promise."

"Why?"

"Never mind why. Just do it," Grandpa growled.

"I promise.".

"Good," he nodded. "Nothing there for you anyway but a bunch of sad losers sitting around wishing things were different. Don't you be a loser, Palmer! Don't you sit around pining for things you can't do anything about. The past is the past. Let it stay there."

Grandpa pulled an ace from the bottom of a row, set it up high.

"Nothing there for you but pain. A reservation is a cavity, like in your teeth, only this one's in your soul. Can't no dentist fix it, and when you're there, your soul aches all the time. It's no good for anyone, and don't let anyone tell you otherwise."

A truck's horn blared at One-Shot, whose speed had dropped considerably. The semi roared by him, and he swerved into the emergency lane, his tires jolting as he powered over the rumble strip. Pebbles crunched under rubber as he squealed to a stop, watching the taillights of the truck speed off into the wilds.

He scrubbed his smoky hand across his face, reached out a hand to feel Grandpa's urn. He ran his palm over the lid and made sure Grandpa was still sealed inside.

The highway behind him sat flat. The headlights in the distance shimmered like they were underwater, reflecting off the dry blacktop. He chugged the rest of his can of Dr. Pepper, crushed it, and tossed the empty in the back seat. Though there was nothing out here, he couldn't bring himself to litter. He'd clear out all his garbage at the next gas station.

When he'd gotten his bearings, resituated himself in the present, he pulled back onto the highway and stomped the gas pedal to the floor. The back of his skull pressed against the headrest as if he was blasting off into outer space.

"How many Gs you think I'm pulling?" One-Shot asked.

*One. There's only one G on planet Earth.*

"Where's your sense of imagination?"

One-Shot checked the gauges on his dashboard and eased off the gas pedal, relaxing as the RPMs of his vehicle eased into an acceptable range.

"Sorry to break my promise, Grandpa."

By way of apology, he sang Grandpa his song again, his mind wandering to the past once more. His time machine took him…only it never took him any place he wanted to go.

**Yesterday**

The fridge had been stocked with cheap domestic beer in silver cans. Turns out Mom had bought a full rack, had only been waiting for the mountains to turn blue. Ordinarily, One-Shot was of the opinion parents and kids shouldn't party together, but this was as close as they would get to a funeral, so he guessed it was okay. Justified, he grabbed a beer, popped the top, and prepared to be Arnold for the next few hours.

In the living room, Raven and Mom sat on the couch poring over old photo albums.

Arnold tried to nurse his beer, but it seemed like every time he looked down, the damn can he held was empty. He'd rather be drinking whiskey, but Grandpa didn't allow it in his house. He just said he'd spent too much of his life trying to be civilized to allow himself to transform back into a savage under the bewitching glamour of hard alcohol. He always said shit like that, real folksy, wise shit, like he was a medicine man or something.

For the most part, Mom held it together. Oh, the tears still flowed, but they were punctuated with bouts of amusing memories and followed by laughter. She was cycling, like one of those old dolls with the pull string. *Yank.* Remember when Grandpa tried to deep fry a turkey? *Yank.* Hahaha! *Yank.* I can't believe he's gone. *Yank.* He always said he was going to stop celebrating Thanksgiving all together. Remember that? Said it was a punishment made up by the white man to remind us that we were fucking nice to these pieces of shit when they had nothing. *Yank.* Oh, God. What are we going to do for Thanksgiving?

And so on and—*burp*—so forth.

Mom flipped a page in an old album. To Arnold, the photos were magic, small windows into the past. He used to flip through those photo albums when he got sad, when he was lonely and forgotten and needed a reminder that even though his parents had left, they still loved him. He would flip open the album and stare at the pictures, wonder who was on the other side of the camera, who was off to the side, making silly faces at them to get them to smile.

In his family, it was guaranteed that if someone was having their picture taken, they wouldn't smile unless you tricked one out of them. It was important to be stoic in pictures. You didn't want your photo albums to wind up in some sort of weird garage sale when you died, and some white motherfucker bought it and saw all these smiling Indians. That wouldn't do at all. That would rob them of their magic, of their mystique, and fuck, sometimes that's all Indians had.

He was practicing his serious face, when his mother asked him about her...about Sadie. "What happened between you two?"

The question came out of nowhere, surprised the hell out of him. Part of him got angry—that quick-lightning, drunk kind of anger that sprung up on people at the oddest moments. But he was only two sheets, so the feeling didn't take, died out like a match in the rain, leaving behind embarrassment like the lingering stench of sulfur on the wind.

"We just grew apart," he said.

His mother closed the photo album in her lap while Raven grabbed a silver can, tilted it back, spilled a little beer down the sides of her mouth, and then disappeared into the kitchen. His mother gave her a look like, *What the fuck do you know that you're not telling me?* Then, she turned back to Arnold.

"But why?" she asked.

"It happens, you know? Sometimes people are just different."

He could tell his answer wasn't good enough for her. Painting with a broad brush when she wanted fine details would never suffice. But the story of him and Sadie wasn't solely his for the telling, so he held back. Maybe one day, when it didn't hurt so much. Though, he didn't know why it was so important to protect his mother from the truth. Maybe a part of him, deep-down, still wanted her approval. Or maybe a part of him was plain embarrassed. He'd tried so hard, before and after, to keep it from ripping Sadie and himself apart. He would have had better luck holding the sun in place.

Raven appeared again, a silver can in her hand, and he noticed how steady she walked and the lack of flushed cheeks. Based upon the way she carried herself, she was maybe one-sheet. She was good like that, never got too far gone. When she did, her emotions came out, big time, and she didn't hold back. Had laid into Arnold more than once for all the mistakes he'd made in his life. "You're the one with the brains!" she'd yell at him. "Why don't you start acting like it?"

Before he could bring up her light drinking, Mom flipped to a picture of One-Shot at his high school graduation. "Have you given any thought to going back to college?" his mom asked.

Arnold shook his head, started playing with his hands. He knew he danced in a minefield now. A single wrong answer to one of Mom's questions and shit would get real. Mom didn't like lies. She wielded the truth like a fucking samurai and expected everyone else to do the same, whether it split your guts open or not.

Mom sighed. He could hear the disappointment in it, working its way from her heart into her lungs and finally into her exhaled breath.

But fuck, it was his life. He ought to be able to do what he wanted with it.

"Are you still bartending?" she asked.

Raven's eyes, went big, and she put the can of Coors Light up to her lips, probably more to keep from reacting than because she wanted a sip of beer he'd bet.

"Yeah. Most nights."

His mom nodded, and he figured something was wrong. He wondered if she was playing him into a trap. When he was younger, he'd spent much of one summer trying to trap squirrels in the backyard. He'd found a big cardboard box, tossed a bunch of roasted, salted peanuts on the ground, and waited out of sight with a piece of twine clutched in his hands. He caught a bunch of squirrels that way—figured it made him more Indian. Grandpa wouldn't get him a bow and arrow— said there was no need for it.

Right now, under his mother's scrutiny, he felt like one of those trapped squirrels, happily nibbling away at a pile of processed peanuts, oblivious to the trap hanging above him. Any second now, she was gonna pull on that twine-wrapped stick and bring the box crashing down on him.

Rather than let it happen, Arnold rose from the couch and fled to the porch. A cigarette found his hands, and even though his bladder threatened to explode in his jeans, he managed to light it. The sun was turning orange now, the air cooling to an almost tolerable eighty degrees. The smells of summer floated on the air, mingling with his cigarette smoke as it drifted across Grandpa's gravel lawn like a cloud of gnats. The heat allowed the smoke to hang like a ghost, gave it an almost flowery air.

His phone buzzed in his pocket. "Fucking fuck," he mumbled with the butt of the cigarette clamped between his lips. On the phone, the icon for his email popped up. He unlocked it, read through the email. *Another client.*

He tucked his phone away, made a mental note to call them later, when he wasn't all fucked up. He flicked the cigarette over the side of the porch, but didn't look to see where it landed. An older lady walking a thick dog with a smashed face shook her head, and it took all his patience not to snap at her.

*Yeah. Better call her tomorrow.* Clients didn't grow on trees, not for what he did. Inside the house, his mother had transitioned from two to three sheets. He didn't know how it was possible. When he left, she'd been fine—or fine-ish. Now she was all tears and wailing. A quick transition—one that always freaked him out. But that was how alcohol was, right? One minute you're fine, and the next minute you're breaking out the windows on your girlfriend's car and riding to the police station.

His mother stood and seemed to groan in mild pain. Watching her slowly rise, the thickness of her thighs, the pillows of her ass, he understood she was getting older. This might be the best it would get for her. As much as he'd loved Grandpa, Arnold knew they would have to go through all this shit again in the near future when his parents passed away.

Mom shambled across the room, her arms held out to him while Raven looked on, swaying in the kitchen. His mother enveloped him, and he squirmed underneath his skin, not quite feeling like he deserved such affection. He squeezed her back, and Raven came in like a ghost, appearing out of nowhere, wrapping her arms around him and Mom, trapping Arnold in the middle. He smelled their shampoo, the wetness of their tears, and their grief—which didn't smell all that different from summer tobacco smoke hanging in the air.

"You'll take him home?" his mother asked.

Because she was crying, because she grieved, because he was drunk, he said, "Yes."

"They'll want you there," she sniffed. "You'll have to be careful."

*Four sheets. She's four sheets and out of her mind.* "Okay, Mom."

"You have to watch out for the Whistle Man. He likes to play games."

Above her head, with his mother's patchy hair pressed against his chin, he grimaced. He wondered how she had gotten so wasted, so fast. Hell, he didn't even think it was possible for someone to get four sheets on Coors Light without mainlining the stuff. She stepped back from him, grabbed him by the upper arms, and looked up into his face with eyes that made him ache in the soul. She said nothing, releasing him after a moment.

Mom wandered away, putting her arm out to steady herself as she stumbled up the steps to the second floor. She climbed as if her sadness weighed her down. Perhaps the memory of Grandpa dragged along behind her, so heavy Arnold was surprised it didn't leave furrows on the stair carpet. When she disappeared, the two siblings whispered as if they were eight years old again, when the music stopped and the snoring started. For as bad as she could be when she was drunk, you did not want to wake Mom up after she fell asleep. So, they sat together, their foreheads inches apart.

The survival habits of children are special things, pure and long-lasting, even into adulthood. As an adult, they remained a part of you, like the scar on your chin, which you might only notice a few times a year, even though it was always there. Some asshole might point it out, say, "Hey, what's up with that scar on your chin?" Most people would just shrug and ignore the question, because it was their scar. It was their business and fuck the person who asked. *What's up with you being such a nosy little bitch?*

"What the fuck is the Whistle Man?" Arnold asked, an amused smile breaking across his mouth as he tried to prevent himself from breaking into laughter.

Raven didn't laugh though. Her eyes were big and serious, made him want to get another beer out of the fridge.

"I don't know," she rasped. "She's been weird all day."

"What're you talkin' about? She's just sad is all."

"I don't think so. I think it's something more."

"Man, you need to quit drinking," Arnold scoffed.

"I haven't been drinking."

"Wha—?"

"Well, I had one, but you know, the rest was water," explained Raven.

Arnold picked up his sister's can and took a sip. Metallic, lukewarm water poured down the back of his throat, and he spit it across the wooden floor. "What the hell, Raven?"

"Shhh," Raven hissed.

He handed the can back to her, a frown on his face. He didn't like to be tricked, especially not by his older sister. "What's up with you?"

Raven sat back on the couch. The material was November-sky gray, somewhat ratty. Grandpa had never been one to splurge on things. If it was broken, he would replace it. But until that happened, he would sit on his furniture until the legs came off.

"Something's wrong with Mom."

Arnold opened his mouth to protest, but Raven sped on.

"You don't know her like I do. Something is off. When I talked to her on the phone, all she could do was ask about you. She kept asking if you were going to be here."

"What's so weird about that?"

"You wanna know what's fucking weird about that?"

"I said it, didn't I?"

"She said, 'Now it's Arnold's turn.'"

"Turn for what?"

Raven threw her hands in the air and cocked her head to the side, as if to say, *See, I fucking told you.* "I have no fucking clue."

"She's just fucked up, man. Grief does weird shit."

"You're so fucking clueless," Raven said. Arnold's head rocked back as Raven slapped her palm off his forehead. The sound echoed like the report of a cap gun. Their heads snapped to look at the stairs leading to the second floor. For a moment, they became children again. They held their breath and waited for Mom to come stumbling down the steps to lay into them for disturbing her sleep, as she'd done when they were both younger. One-Shot's heart beat in his ears like a drum.

When she didn't appear, Raven said. "You didn't even ask where home was, dipshit."

"Wha—?" he asked, his thoughts sluggish. He was sure a red mark was growing on his forehead from Raven's slap.

"Home? Here. Duh," he sputtered. *How drunk does she think I am?*

"It's tough having all the emotions *and* all the brains," Raven said.

Arnold held his hand out to the side, made a jerking-off motion.

"This isn't home for Grandpa. It never was."

"Oh, shit."

"Yep. Siletz."

"I can't go to Siletz," Arnold whined. "I don't even know where it is."

"You already told mom you'd go. *I'm* certainly not doing it."

"She's not going to remember," Arnold said, waving off the prospect of having to go to Siletz, Oregon, their tribal reservation, which was smaller than a postage stamp according to Grandpa.

Raven smirked. "You know that's not how it works."

Arnold leaned back on the gray, threadbare couch and sighed. Mom might be a drunk, but she wasn't a blackout drunk. For most people, it worked the other way. But she remembered everything she said when she was wasted. Even worse, she remembered everything everyone else said as well. Hell, she had a better memory when she was three sheets than she did when she was stone-cold.

"Fucking Siletz?"

"Fucking Siletz," Raven confirmed.

"What is that, like a two-thousand-mile drive?"

Raven picked up her phone and typed in a search. "2697.1 miles," she announced.

"My car won't even make it."

Raven shrugged like it wasn't her problem.

"Why the fuck do I have to go to Siletz?"

"He wants to be buried with Grandma."

*This just keeps getting better and better.* "Do they have a plot in the cemetery or something?"

"That's a *you* problem," Raven said.

"Don't you wanna go?" Arnold asked.

"I said my goodbyes. He's gone now. What happens to the body is just…math."

Arnold knew Raven hated math. She used the word in all sorts of ways. When she didn't have enough money to pay her rent, that was math. When someone she liked stopped calling her, that was math. When she started putting on weight around her middle, that was also math. As far as Raven was concerned, math was a force of nature. No reason to worry about it.

They fell silent, and Arnold began to imagine the road spreading out before him, the entirety of the continental U.S. flying by underneath the wheels of his Honda Accord. *Goddamn car isn't going to make it.*

"There's money, I guess," Raven said.

His ears perked up.

"Yeah. Eight grand for burial expenses—from the tribe."

"Well, yeah, I'm gonna need some of that."

"What? Being a gigolo doesn't pay enough?"

"I'm not a gigolo."

Raven shrugged, not willing to get into a fight about it. They already knew where the other stood on the issue. She hated that he was chucking bastards into the world, but he was doing his part for his tribe, trying to insure it didn't disappear via basic attrition.

Arnold sighed and ran a hand through his hair. "Fuuuucckkk."

Raven smiled then. "I'd go with you—"

"Yeah?"

"...but I'm pregnant."

"Fuck you," he spat.

Raven bent her face into an approximation of a smile, one that didn't touch her eyes. "I am."

"No." The thought of his sister having a child was revolting. "Is it his?"

Raven nodded, and in the dim light of the living room, he noted the tears in her eyes.

"Is that why you're not together?"

She nodded again.

*Fuck. What a mess.*

He fell silent then, his own traumas rising up and threatening to devour him. But this wasn't about him, was it? It was about Raven. "Does Mom know?" He realized how stupid the question sounded once it came out of his mouth. "Of course, she doesn't. If she did, it's all she would have been talking about."

They lapsed into an uncomfortable silence, unsaid words hanging between them, things they should be saying. But they had been stunted, trained to keep their feelings inside, so they let the silence drag on and on.

Arnold lifted a hand and placed it on her shoulder. She held her head down—embarrassed, worried...he didn't know what. Her hair hung down and hid her face.

"You gonna keep it?" he asked, because he could. Because he knew about that stuff. Because he knew it was an option and maybe she just needed someone to tell her it was okay.

She shrugged.

"Stop fucking shrugging. Just talk."

"I don't know," Raven said. "Could be good, yeah?"

"Could be," he conceded. "Could be bad, too."

Tears plopped on the faded gray couch, turning the threadbare material a dark charcoal. Maybe when they dried, the couch would be stronger, covered in a layer of sorrow-laden salt. Might get a couple more months out of the damn thing if they kept crying.

"Arnold?"

"Yeah."

"You'd make a shitty uncle."

He shoved her lightly, smiling. "Fuck you. I'd be a great uncle."

"I don't want some kid of mine learning the gigolo arts from Uncle Hobag."

"I'd take it to Penguins games, Steelers games... Probably not the Pirates, but maybe once."

"Yeah? With what money? How many dead grandpas you got?"

Then they were back to their sorrow. It fell over them, a blanket thrown over a birdcage. They sat studying the threads of the blanket, their own personal memories of a relationship, rich and rewarding, one they'd never experience again.

"I gotta go," Arnold said. The blanket was too heavy, too suffocating. He had to get out.

Raven nodded. She knew his ways and wouldn't beg him to stay.

As he reached the door, he turned and looked over his shoulder. "If you need anything, let me know, even if you just need to talk."

Raven nodded. "Love you," she said.

"Love you, too."

And then he was gone.

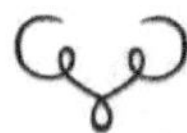

The night rolled on and the highway morphed into a different plane of existence.

Grandpa fell silent and the song died on One-Shot's lips. Napping probably. The elderly did that sometimes.

This left One-Shot alone with his thoughts. Locked into solitude, the mistakes of his life bubbled up before him like an agitated toad's eyes in a witch's cauldron. College... He had been the first person in the family to go. Grandpa, who might have been the smartest member of the family, had carved a career out of spit and duct tape, latching on with the FBI at some point. But he never told them what he did or how he got the job. In the end, Grandpa had set his past to the side once he retired. Whenever One-Shot or Raven would ask him about his past, he claimed it was all "classified," and he'd have to kill them if he told them. One-Shot suspected Grandpa just didn't want to talk about it.

One-Shot understood the sentiment. He was not one for talking about anything. One-Shot preferred the past to stay buried in the dark cemetery of his mind where he kept his failures and disappointments. However, traveling along the road to the West, with no stereo, no mindless drone of music, talk radio, or annoying commercials, he was left digging up the skeletons in his mental graveyard.

College was one of those skeletons. Against his grandpa's wishes, he'd fallen in love before he got the pieces of his life put in place. A lawyer. That's what he told everyone he was going to be. He had the grades, had the willpower, and had the time. For years, he kept his head down, always listening to the voice in the back of his head, an echo of Grandpa. "Don't you fall in love, Palmer!"

Easier said than done. He'd met Sadie his junior year. In between his classes, he caught her smoking in a courtyard. They'd struck up a conversation, found each other palatable, and soon after, they were shacking up whenever they got the chance.

He'd meant it to be temporary, a relationship of convenience. But it had turned into more than that. His grades suffered. His heart beat down his brain and turned it into a confused pile of Jell-O rattling around in his skull. Cs and Ds were technically passing at the University of Pittsburgh, but they weren't good enough to maintain his scholarship. With three quarters of his education done, he found himself at a crossroads, unable to pay for the rest of his schooling, and unlikely to have grades good enough to get into law school even if he managed to finish his undergraduate work.

If Sadie had cared, if she had given two shits about anything more than who he was, he might have stuck it out, might have worked two jobs, saved up the money, and paid his own way through school. But she didn't care. She wasn't like that. It didn't matter to her what job he had or if he was just some bum on the street. She only cared that he was who he was—Arnold.

Of course, when he'd dropped out of school, he settled the weight of failure on his shoulders like a cape. He let it pull him down into the swamp of his own self-pity. One-Shot distanced himself from his family because he couldn't face them. He'd been the hope, the one who was going to make it. When he didn't, he felt like he'd let them down, even though he knew they still loved him in their own way. He lost the shine, stopped being the golden boy, and became the man made of lead, heavy and immovable, a handy bit of reverse-alchemy there.

He started working long nights as a bartender, rolling in at three in the morning, crawling into bed next to Sadie, reeking of booze. His life could have gone on like that forever, and he would have been happy. Probably would have died in a couple decades from a busted liver, but hey, what good is a life not lived?

Then, one drunken night he'd crawled into bed, found Sadie ready and willing. A few weeks later, Sadie started throwing up. Her pale skin turned paler, and she disappeared up to the grocery store and came back with a stack of pregnancy tests.

One-Shot didn't know what to do or say. Was he supposed to be happy? Was this just fate? In those days, One-Shot liked to blame everything on fate, but he knew it was more than that. It was a drunken decision on his part. He knew Sadie didn't want kids and was getting close to finishing her own education. While his grades had suffered because of their love, Sadie's had never wavered, and she was on the verge of graduation, getting ready to go into medical school to become a physical therapist.

*Why would she want to be with me?*

A part of him wanted her to come out of the bathroom with a smile on her face, to burst through the door like the fucking Kool-Aid Man waving around a positive test. If she did that, he'd have known everything would be alright.

Unfortunately, Sadie didn't come out like that. Instead, she'd slunk from the bathroom as if her life was over. She didn't even talk to him. He had to go into the bathroom and dig the pregnancy test out of the garbage to see for himself.

They lay in bed then, silent, the world spinning around him as if it was three in the morning and he'd just finished his shift.

"You wanna keep it?" he asked.

"I don't know."

More silence. Deep breathing. She rolled over on the bed, turned her back to him.

"I'm okay with whatever you want to do," he said, though he wanted to keep it. He wanted to keep the life they'd made together and could only imagine how awesome a child that was the best parts of the both of them could be.

Sadie's response was to wrap her arms around herself.

Then the bunnies hit the windshield.

They came across the road, leaping and bounding without a care in the world. Hundreds of them, so many that One-Shot assumed something was herding them, chasing them out of the dark fields and onto the highway. He was so lost in his thoughts, he didn't react until the first one thundered against the grill of his car. Then he plowed through them, screaming as his car mowed them down by the dozens. Some of the four-legged bodies flipped up over his hood, and in a brief flash of light, he made eye contact with one of the victims, locked onto its strangely human eye and the fear contained within. His stomach dropped.

One-Shot screamed as he slammed on his brakes. He closed his eyes, gripped the steering wheel. The herd thundered away from the car, leaving him alone in the night, parked in the middle of the highway on the western edge of Iowa amid the wreckage of bodies. Without opening his eyes, he let the car inch forward, refusing to see the carnage he'd wreaked. After a few seconds, with the fear of winding up in a ditch growing in his mind, he forced his eyes open and found the pools of his headlights had turned red. Smears of blood and clumps of fur clung to his windshield.

*They know you're coming. They're testing you,* Grandpa said.

When One-Shot turned his head to the side, he thought he saw Grandpa sitting next to him—just for a moment. But then he blinked, and Grandpa was gone, replaced by the brass urn, the lid still secured with duct tape. The seat belt had kept it from spilling to the floor when he'd slammed on the brakes.

One-Shot wiped at his eyes and thought maybe he should pull over, catch a couple of winks. If he hadn't been busy choking on fear, he would have. The mind, when isolated, was capable of amazing things. In this instance, it conjured for One-Shot a herd of vengeful bunnies appearing out of the night, converging on him in his sleep. They would tear their way through the garbage bag window, hop inside, and nibble him to death for what he'd done to their family members. Rationally, he knew bunnies taking revenge was out of the realm of possibility, but he was all on his own out here. While he had never heard of carnivorous bunny attacks in the rational world, maybe that was because they only went after poor motherfuckers who slept along the side of the highway.

He couldn't risk it. With his headlights glowing red, he continued down the highway, hoping no cop spotted his vehicle and mistook him for one of those psychos who plowed through crowds of people because they were going insane or couldn't get laid. Hell, where would he even find a crowd in Iowa?

With his heart hammering in his chest and his eyes trying not to see the severed, bloody foreleg sitting on his hood, he drove onward. One-Shot hoped for a gas station or perhaps an all-night car wash, though he doubted such a thing existed out here.

To calm his nerves, he reached for his cigarettes, his medicine, tried to think about something nice as he let the cigarette burn between his fingers. *Jane Anthony...*

He looked at the message one more time and then checked his email. The subject line read: "Jane Anthony: Re: Natural Insemination." He clicked on the email and read the woman's message.

> *Dear Arnold Yeager,*
>
> *I am contacting you about the service of Natural Insemination you offer. I am extremely interested and would love to discuss this opportunity with you.*
>
> *Here is some information about myself so you can see I am serious. I oversee a large produce shipping company based out of Ohio. I make a seven-figure salary. Any child I have will be well-cared and provided for. Though my job is busy and time-consuming, I still have the time to raise a child and could see myself retiring in a few short years. Being this successful has come with some drawbacks, namely finding the time to build a family in a more traditional manner.*

*As the CEO of a company, I encounter and interact with all cultures. The child born of this opportunity will be raised with knowledge of their Indigenous heritage.*

*Sincerely,*
*Jane Anthony*
*CEO Global Produce Co. Unlimited*

She said all the right things and knew all the code words he wanted to hear. One-Shot didn't want to just impregnate women, he wanted to create more Native Americans, specifically members of his tribe. It was a necessity. While Corey and his other buddies thought he'd just found a clever way to dip his wick, it wasn't about that for One-Shot. It was about the continuation of his people.

Though he had grown up off the reservation, in a city 2,697.1 miles away, he knew his history. Grandpa had made sure of that and impressed upon him the unfairness of the world, the traumas of history and their impact upon the tribe as he knew it. He wasn't a perfect man, but he wanted to make sure One-Shot knew these things, knew why sometimes Grandpa came home with a half-rack of Rainier and cried at the kitchen table while playing old records.

The American government was the enemy, always would be. They played the long game, and this is what had cost the tribes back in the day. After figuring out a war against the tribes would be costly and bloody, they came up with an ingenious plan: just have them breed themselves out. Once a drop of non-Indian blood was introduced into the tribe, the doomsday clock started ticking. Once you became…impure, there was only one endgame, the complete extinction of Indigenous people. One-Shot stood at the edge of that outcome, a generation removed from his entire tribe's extinction. Unless he married someone with more Indian blood than himself, his children would be the last generation of Indians in his family. This was a crime to him, every bit as wrong as the massacres and the smallpox blankets or the Indian schools they were forced to attend where people were beaten for speaking their languages and often thrown into nameless graves when they died.

One-Shot's case was not a special one. Most of the tribe was in the same boat. When the tribal newspaper came in the mail, the people inside all had white and Latino surnames. It was only a matter of time before they were all gone. This the government had planned. *Oh, sure Red Man, we'll give you all these cool benefits, set aside some land for you to live on, even allow you to "govern" yourselves… But you must agree to this one, simple, teeny-tiny, little change. We call it Blood Quantum.*

*What's that?* the Red Man asked.

*Oh, that's where we measure how much of a Native American you are with fractions. So if Joe Monosyllabic gets with Jane White, next thing you know you have a kid who is one-half Native American. Joe Jr. gets with another Jane White, then his kids are down to being one-fourth Native American. Now, if Joe the Third gets with a Jane White, they're offspring will be one-eighth Native American, which really isn't that Native American to begin with, so we don't really have to pay them all the things we agreed to in the treaties. They're screwed.*

*But wait a second,* the Red Man asked, *what about all those one-drop rules for African Americans?*

*Oh...those... Well, you see, it's all about umm...you know, limiting the amount of people who can be white, workforces, cheap labor... You know, above the level stuff. I mean, in the end it's all about money and what profits the government more. We're not racist...not really.*

With the imaginary conversation running through his head for the umpteenth time, One-Shot scribbled down her phone number and gave her a call.

"Hello?" a woman answered.

"Good afternoon. My name is Arnold Yeager. You sent me an email yesterday." He didn't mention the subject, as he knew some people got weird when on the phone.

"Yes, yes. Good to hear from you, Mr. Yeager."

"I wanted to touch base with you and set up a meet and greet."

This was a necessary step. He might want to keep his tribe going, but he wasn't trying to birth Indian kids with complete nutjobs. The world was hard enough without having to grow up with a parent like that.

"I'm a little busy right now," Jane said. "But later this week, I might have something open on Thursday evening. Let's say six o'clock?"

"Six works for me. Where would you like to meet?"

Any time worked for One-Shot. He used to keep regular hours, used to actually work a job as a bartender, but he'd ditched all that when he found his new calling.

"I'm thinking my place would be good. This isn't really the type of conversation I'd like to have over drinks in public."

"I hear that. Shoot me your address, and I'll meet you at six o'clock on Thursday. We can go over all the particulars of the procedure." He liked to call it a procedure. It made him feel like a doctor. "Then we'll see if we're a match."

He jotted down the address, wrote down what to say to the doorman, said his goodbyes, and leaned back on his couch.

One-Shot's apartment was small, the furniture functional and basic. When people came over, they described it as sterile, empty, which was just fine for him. He didn't want people in his space, didn't need them getting up in his business. Sterile and empty suited One-Shot. He fell over on his side and curled into a ball, wondering how long it would take him to drive to Siletz, Oregon.

Though he didn't want to admit it, he was nervous about visiting the reservation. He kept wondering if he was Native American enough. Shit, half his friends had said, "I don't even think of you as Native American" at one point or another. Some of them used the word "Indigenous," but he hated that fucking word. Made him and other Natives sound like fucking plant life. Fucking *corn* is indigenous to the Americas, not people.

Either way, he knew he wasn't like one of those turquoise, smudging-his-apartment type of motherfuckers. He had never ridden a horse, never danced around a fire or beat on a drum outside of elementary school music class. He knew about all that shit, had read it secondhand, but wasn't willing to lie to himself and pretend like that's who he was. Consequently, he was anxious about going to a place where they did all that shit. Would he be out of place in Siletz? Would he walk around and see a dozen motherfuckers who looked just like him strutting around town?

Or would they take one look at him, raz him out of town, call him a Pretendian? Perhaps this was the only time in his life where he could agree with the blood quantum rule. If they fucked with him, he could hold out his forearm, slide a razorblade through his flesh, pull out one of those slides from science class, and have the other members of his tribe examine it under a microscope. They would look and look, examining and measuring, and then of course, because they all had to pretend like your blood mattered, they would say, "Oh yeah, I see…seven-sixteenths. How the hell'd you manage that?"

"It's a long story," he'd say, and then they'd dance around the fire like brothers.

*Ridiculous,* he thought as his eyelids began to drift over his eyes.

His eyes snapped open as Grandpa's words rolled through his head once more, pulling him back to the present. *They know you're coming.*

"Who the fuck are *they*?" He blew smoke out the window. "And why the fuck are *they* testing me?"

But Grandpa wasn't talking now, or ever really.

It would be some time before a gas station loomed out of the darkness, an island of bright fluorescent sanity allowing One-Shot's heartbeat to return to normal. In the meantime, he tried not to think about the rabbits, choosing instead to dig in his cemetery of failures.

Bouncing back and forth from current horror to past horrors, he made his way into Nebraska. Cornstalks grown mid-summer-height blocked off vision of anything else. The world rolled on, flat and lifeless. One-Shot willed the sun to rise. The sun didn't oblige.

After another thirty minutes, a town appeared, its lights oranging the sky in the distance. One-Shot took the exit, his turn signal flashing pink in the night.

He pulled up to the pumps and figured he'd fill up while he was here.

"Jeeeeezus," the gas station attendant said after he'd pulled into the truck stop. "What happened to you?"

"Hit a herd of rabbits out on the highway."

"A herd you say?"

"Musta been hundreds of 'em."

The attendant side-eyed him, and One-Shot could tell the attendant didn't believe him. He reached into the passenger side of his vehicle and pulled Grandpa free. Inside the gas station, he bought several bottles of water and snagged some napkins from the dispenser sitting next to an ancient hot-roller with leathery hot dogs spinning to infinity. He stuffed a dozen of the napkins in his pockets, despite the glare from the cashier.

Outside, he placed Grandpa back in the car. With napkins in hand, he walked around his car, picking off chunks of flesh and fur, and finally removing the stubborn foreleg that had clung to the hood of his vehicle for the last thirty miles. "Sorry, pal," he said as he placed the leg in the garbage can, the gas station attendant looking on with revulsion. One-Shot shrugged apologetically at the man.

He dumped the water on his car, watching as the blood ran off the sides and onto the pavement. He wetted a few napkins and went at his headlights, his stomach doing backflips. Just as he threw the last of his bloody napkins into the garbage nestled between the pumps, a cop pulled up, and immediately, One-Shot went into paranoia mode.

Though he had committed no crime, hadn't even had a drink, he was sure the cops would hassle him. But they did nothing of the sort. Instead, they parked in front of the convenience store and headed inside without even looking at him.

With his panic lessened, he walked around to the gas pump, slid his debit card home, and began filling his tank.

A sharp whistle broke the night air. His head spun to the side, and he beheld a man with silver-black hair spilling from under a black hat with a broad brim. The whistling man stood leaning against the bricks of the convenience store, one leg cocked up. Brown cowboy boots, worn and scuffed, peeked out from under faded jeans the color of a spring sky, his upper torso covered in a Pendleton-patterned wool jacket. The man's thin lips shifted and the whistling transformed, becoming a haunting, lilting song.

One-Shot locked eyes with the man for a moment. They were beady, black things—cricket eyes. The man nodded at him, and One-Shot jumped as the gas pump clicked to a stop with a metallic clang. He hung up the nozzle and left without taking his receipt.

The whistling man watched him the entire way, a queer smile spreading across his lips. The hair stood up on the back of One-Shot's neck.

"I'm fucking losing it."

He flopped in his car and turned the key in the ignition, fully expecting his car not to start, as that's the way things seemed to be going.

Despite the broken window and too many miles, the Honda Accord purred to life. He shifted into drive, but resisted the urge to peel out of the parking lot. Nothing brought a cop running like the potential of someone trying to flee. In the rearview mirror, he saw the whistling man abandon his comfy lean and start walking across the paved apron of the gas station. The odd smile was still glued to the whistling man's face.

When he hit the freeway on-ramp, he gunned the engine.

## Chapter 2: On the Road – Day Two

The miles sped by, the road molting from black to blue to orange to gray in the progressing dawn. By the time noon rolled around, the pavement was a blinding white, the yellow lines the only sign of color. With the day's return, a sense of normalcy and calm reinvigorated One-Shot. In those wee hours of the morning before the sun's ascension, he had quaked with fear, wondering what was in store for him next. Whatever nightmares were out there in the darkness stayed hidden, leaving him with only the specters of crushed bunnies, whistling men, and his past.

His car ran hot in the summer sun. For fuel, he slugged down warm cans of Dr. Pepper and choked down jerky. He drove the speed limit now, wondering how many miles his car could take. He'd put a lot of wear and tear on the Accord over the last day, hundreds of miles already, with twenty more hours of driving to go. By his calculations, he was little more than halfway across the country.

Already his body rebelled. He'd pulled his wallet from his jeans some time ago. The small, leather billfold had steadily built pressure underneath his ass, causing him to sit crooked and producing a dull ache that climbed up his back and radiated down into his left leg. His pelvis felt like it was going to crack at any moment.

Maybe on the way back he'd take it slower, stop in a town or two and have a drink. But for now, he was on a quest, and there was a time limit. Who knew how long Grandpa's spirit would remain with the urn? The last thing he wanted was for Grandpa to get bored and find himself lost in... A sign declaring the current nondescript city as Cheyenne, Wyoming passed him by. He couldn't leave Grandpa in Cheyenne! One-Shot didn't know a damn thing about Cheyenne, and he guessed Grandpa didn't either…unless.

"You ever been to Cheyenne, Grandpa?" No reply. "Any of your FBI buddies retire out here?"

Only One-Shot's grumbling stomach replied. He spotted a sign for a burger joint that proclaimed itself as royalty, a king among fast-food places. He pulled into the castle of burgers, eased himself into the drive-through lane.

The menu gleamed bright, the morning sun bouncing off the protective plastic and stabbing him in the eyes. *I'll have to get some sunglasses at the next gas station.* But for now—food. He ordered a flame-broiled Doozy, a large order of fries, and another Dr. Pepper. If he let his caffeine levels bottom out, he'd fall asleep while driving, then who would take Grandpa to the cemetery?

After he exited the drive-through, he set the bag of goodies next to Grandpa. "Sorry. Didn't get nothin' for you."

*I'm not hungry anyway.*

With the drink balanced between his knees, and his hands crossed over the top of the steering wheel, he flew down the highway munching on fries, still traveling slower than most of the vehicles who blasted by him, rocking the Accord from side to side in their wake. He didn't care though. *Slow and steady.*

He tossed the empty French fry carton on the passenger-side floorboard, then dug in the bag for the Doozy, a flame-broiled mound of beef covered in American cheese, a piece of lettuce, a tomato, and pickles on a sesame seed bun. Steering with the underside of his forearms, he unwrapped the burger and tried to keep it from dripping all over himself since he hadn't brought a change of clothes along.

In hindsight, he should have stopped home before he left. A change of clothes would be nice. The ones he wore ripened by the minute. He could stop somewhere and buy some clothes, but he didn't feel like walking through a department store with Grandpa under his arm. Someone might accuse him of theft, and then they'd make him open the urn, and he didn't want Grandpa to have to deal with that bullshit.

Maybe after he buried Grandpa he could stop somewhere and re-up. *God, I really am shit at planning.* But he'd wanted to go, to flee the city after…after…

Jane Anthony lived in a swanky part of downtown, in a building that wore its security like a badge of honor. The high-rise apartment building jutted up into the sky, penetrating the glowing gloom of the evening. Not a star in sight. Not here. Not in the city.

The doorman took one look at One-Shot and demanded he sign in and present his driver's license.

"You get a lot of trouble around here?" One-Shot asked as the doorman studied his license.

"Nope, and we aim to keep it that way. Who'd you say you were here to see?"

"Jane Anthony."

The doorman, a thick Yinzer motherfucker with an accent like a barking dog, picked up the phone and dialed a number. "Good evening, Ms. Anthony. Got a man down here, name of Arnold Yeager, says he's here to see you."

The doorman listened for a moment, then handed One-Shot's license back. "Here you go."

One-Shot stuffed the license in his wallet and headed for the elevator doors. He pressed the call button and stood with the doorman's eyes piercing his back, stabbing through his clothes and into his shoulder blades. Some people, you could feel their hate. When the elevator doors opened, he was quick to step inside and sever the piercing gaze.

He pressed the button for the sixth floor, kept his head down lest someone came running up at the last second, necessitating him to make a decision—hold the door or let them close without even trying. No one appeared, and he exhaled as the doors slid shut, the elevator lurching to life. Up he went, praying no one else would get on the elevator.

Without warning, the elevator jerked, the lights flickering. The air in the elevator thickened, and thin beads of alcohol-laced sweat dripped from his pores. He tried to stop sweating through sheer will of his mind, but all that seemed to do was make more sweat spring up. An elevator speaker crackled to life. He jumped, dropping his briefcase to the ground. A bead of sweat dripped from his nose when he bent over to retrieve it.

*Why the fuck is this elevator ride taking so long?*

The sound of a baby emanated from the speaker, punching One-Shot in the guts. Its simple burbles heightened, became more piercing, and then it was wailing in true hideous baby fashion—a primordial cry that made you want to spring to your feet, rush over to the crib, and do anything to get it to stop. He pressed the talk button to cut off the cry.

"Hello?" he asked, wondering if maybe the doorman was fucking with him.

He released the button, and the wailing filled the elevator once more. It intensified in volume, and his eardrums quivered in agony. He dropped his briefcase once more, put his hands to his ears, lest his head explode from the sound.

Then there was an almost imperceptible ding, followed by a small lurch as the elevator stopped. One-Shot screamed as the doors slid open to reveal an elderly woman, bird-thin, wrapped in a tan trench coat. Her hand went to her heart, and she glared daggers at him.

"Sorry," he mumbled as he picked up his briefcase, shoving his free arm through the elevator doors to keep them from closing. For a second, he thought the doors weren't going to open, and he was going to be stuck, his arm trapped between the doors. As an image of his arm being sheared off by the elevator entered his mind, the doors sprung back, and he stepped through quickly. As the doors hummed closed behind him, he leaned against the wall, his eyes closed. *Schizophrenia.* The word danced through his mind. *Is this how it starts?*

He could sit in the hallway all day, wondering and fearing, but sooner or later he was going to have to get about his business.

*And what's with the fucking baby shit?*

He found himself in front of a door, plain like the others. The apartment building was fancy. He'd have to impregnate two women a month just to afford the rent on one of these places. With a shaky hand, he reached up and knocked on the door.

He had to wait a few moments. On the other side, he imagined his prospective client scrambling around, tidying up the place before she came to the door. In his apartment building, you would have been able to hear every movement. One-Shot's building was old, the doors thin and the walls thinner. When his neighbor to the left was busy banging, he could hear the slap of nuts on skin. He didn't want to know what people heard when he had a girl over.

*Sadie…no, not her.*

The door opened at the perfect speed, without rush, not too slow. If a door opening could be described as debonair, that's how he would have described it.

"One-Shot?" the woman asked.

Normally, his clients were a little frumpy, not incapable of finding a man on their own, but just plain enough where people weren't throwing themselves at them. But this woman…my God. *Keep it business.* "Jane?"

She smiled, her lips receding like waves, exposing the beautiful shells of her teeth. "Come on in," she said, a voice like the distant ocean lapping against the shore. Sea-green eyes twinkled.

He stepped across the threshold, butterflies in his belly. She held out her seal-skin hand, and he shook it, enjoying the pale delicateness.

"This way," Jane said, and she led him through her perfectly decorated apartment, not a speck of dust in sight among the expensive furniture. Knick-knacks and souvenirs, all classy and perfect, sat in their destined spaces. Her place seemed like it had been staged for a photo shoot for one of those fancy home magazines. The couch was leather and white, a custom job. It was the type of couch only someone with money would buy. A regular fuck couldn't justify buying something so expensive. All it would take was one spilled glass of wine and the thing would be done for. Then they'd have to sit around, trying to ignore the stain on their five-figure couch, always knowing it was there, always trying to recall the time it was perfect and everything they wanted in life. But in the blink of an eye, it was gone. Such was the way of things.

"Wine?" the woman asked.

Despite his firm "no drinking on duty" policy, the way her voice washed over him picked him up like a crab in the tide, flipped him on his back, and left him helpless, his arms and legs kicking in the air. "Sure," he said.

She returned with a bottle and a thin-stemmed wine glass. Without hesitation, she poured the wine, so near to the white couch that One-Shot had to resist the urge to yell at her, to tell her not to risk it. She poured the wine flawlessly and set the bottle down on a glass table.

"Have a seat," she said, holding the glass out to him.

"Thank you." He took the wine and sat on the couch. She sat across from him in a matching bucket chair.

*Were her lips always that red, or was it the wine?*

The wine tasted like any other, though a little buttery for his taste. He set his glass down with seriousness, concentrating on not shaking and spilling it all over the couch. If he did, he'd lose his whole commission.

"So, Mr. Yeager, tell me about this enterprise of yours."

"Well, I'm a fertilization specialist—naturopathic, of course. My process is guaranteed. As long as everything is in good order on your end, I can provide results after just one session. That's why they call me One-Shot."

The skin around her eyes contracted at the nickname, so he moved past it. "If you decide you want to do business with me, we'll go through all the proper precautions. STI testing, for you and for me, for protection of course. We'll keep track of your cycle and set a date for when you're ovulating. After that…I will inseminate you."

She smiled then, only with the mouth. Her eyes twinkled with intensity. "Tell me about the insemination process," she said, her lips red and full.

"Well, it's a little non-traditional compared to the sort of insemination you'd receive at a doctor's office, but it saves you plenty of money, and my track record speaks for itself. At the agreed upon date, we'll meet, and I will physically deliver the semen."

"You're talking about fucking, One-Shot."

One-Shot shook his head. Normally at these meetings he felt in control, but the sheer power and gravitas of this woman was drowning him, suffocating him. "It's not fucking. For me, this is a business transaction. I keep it as emotionless as possible."

"During sex?"

"Yes."

"What if I don't want it emotionless?"

"Then maybe I'm not the right person for you." He reached forward and picked the wine glass off the table. His lips were suddenly dry. "I am not an escort."

She leaned forward then, the milky swell of her upper breasts visible underneath her V-neck shirt for a half-second as she said, "So you don't enjoy it?"

One-Shot shook his head.

The corner of her mouth curled up, and he could tell she didn't believe him. But she let it drop, leaned back in her chair. "What if it doesn't take?"

He was happy to get back to the more technical questions. Talking about pleasure and emotions always made him crawl in his skin. He wasn't looking for a relationship, wasn't looking to use these people or break their hearts or have them break his. All he wanted to do was get paid, increase his tribe's numbers, and have a drink every now and then. "After a week, we'll take some pregnancy tests, and as of yet, it hasn't been a problem. I have a hundred-percent success rate."

"But what if it doesn't take?"

"It will."

"But if it doesn't."

"Then, I would offer another session for free, as many as you need until the job is done." He chuckled then. "Trust me, it won't be necessary."

She nodded, satisfied by his confidence. "Tell me about your family history."

One-Shot nodded, took another sip of the wine. With 99% of the questions people asked him, he was upfront, honest—perhaps too honest—but when it came to his family history, he had to sort of bend the truth a little bit. No one wanted to know they were potentially getting a kid that would go crazy, have the alcoholism gene running in its blood, or might die early from heart-disease or suicide. "I am half-white, half-native." He wasn't though… He was seven-sixteenths. It was just easier to tell people half. "My mother and father are still alive and doing well in West Virginia." *They run around the woods and get blackout drunk. If there's a finer life out there, I'm not sure what it could be.* "There are scattered instances of heart disease in my family, but with a proper diet, this shouldn't be an issue."

"What about mental health?" Jane asked.

"All good there. The Yeager family is solid."

"Any birth defects? Harelips, Down syndrome, heart on the outside, extra fingers, extra toes?"

"None of that," One-Shot said, happy to be able to tell the truth. He felt like a pilot successfully navigating a ship between two rocks, looking over his shoulder proudly as the two death-bringers receded into the distance.

"Outstanding." Jane took another sip of her wine, savoring it as the wheels turned in her head. "Do you have any children of your own?"

"No. And I'm not planning on it." This was a lie.

"Really?"

"I enjoy the single life, and if I'm going to have a child, I would want the mother involved, and that's just not something

I'm into." Another lie. "But, I feel it's my duty to keep my tribe going." He went into the blood quantum situation then, made himself seem like some sort of saint of genealogy.

Jane ate it up. White people always did. When in doubt, talk about your heritage and your culture. These topics were impregnable shields in which to wrap yourself. So powerful were culture and heritage, only the most audacious of white folks would even think to penetrate those walls, to challenge the things you said under the guise of Indigenousness.

"Fascinating," Jane said when his tirade was done. "So, you're like an Indigenous Johnny Appleseed, but instead of apples, you're spreading your kids around."

One-Shot laughed at the comparison. "Not completely. I mean, he did it for free; I do get paid."

"Yes, I noticed your fee wasn't posted anywhere on your website."

He'd paid some nerd five-hundred-bucks to make the thing. He didn't know how to work it or change it himself, so when the guy had asked him about the price, he'd just said, "Put on there to contact for a quote."

"How much are we talking here?"

*Always ask for more. She looks like she can afford it.* "Twenty thousand."

Where before she had been kind, even charming, Jane Anthony's aspect switched at the first mention of money. She leaned forward, her elbows between her knees, her hands clutching her wine glass. Her V-neck exposed the cleavage between her breasts, making One-Shot swallow. The hollow of her cheek dimpled inward as she sucked on her teeth, preparing for the negotiation.

"Twenty thousand sounds like a little much. Hell, with my insurance, I could go down to the doctor's office and get this all taken care of for the price of a co-pay."

*She's fucking right. But then again, why hadn't she done it already?* "You could. But you don't know what you're getting down there. Oh sure, you can pick out the donor, read their bio, their job description, the things they want to tell you. But I'm right here. I'm an open book. And think about all the benefits. If something were to happen, and you fell on hard times, your child is Native. He or she is entitled to the benefits afforded to tribes—health insurance, help with tuition, food, shelter, dental. Now, is it the greatest insurance in the world? No, it's not. But still, it's nice to know you have something to fall back on, and as a single parent—for now—isn't that worth the price of admission?"

She nodded, seeming to enjoy the process. "It is, but it isn't. One of your former clients told me you did it for ten."

*Shit.* "In some circumstances, when I think someone will make a great parent and they're a little short on cash, I make exceptions." He looked around Jane Anthony's palatial apartment, took it in, and tinkered with his words in his mind so as to flatter and not insult. "Looking at this beautiful home you have here, I can see you're a lady of some means. For a woman of your stature and success, twenty thousand seems like a bargain."

Jane Anthony's eyebrow raised. He could tell she was impressed by his tactics, respected him a little more. One-Shot was good at impressing people at first. If she spent a few more hours with him though, she'd see right through his armor, his defenses, his platitudes, crack open his shell and discover the soft-bodied mollusk that had washed up on her shore.

"Fifteen," she spat before polishing off the last of her wine.

One-Shot smiled. Fifteen was more than he usually got, so he stood up and held out his hand. "Fifteen it is."

She stood and shook, sealing the deal.

"Let's talk dates and deposit," said One-Shot.

From there, One-Shot went through the usual rigamarole, locking down a date eight weeks out just to make sure he didn't contract HIV from his last client. The woman wrote him a check to cover the two-thousand-dollar down payment, and when the bottle was done, and Jane Anthony stopped running her hand along his thigh, he rose, bid her a good night, and saw himself out. It was a hard thing to do. Part of him wanted to run back in there, rip her clothes off, and have a good old time, but with his luck, he'd knock her up then and there and cost himself a payday. Besides, he was a professional.

Outside her apartment, he felt like a man who had come up for air after being underwater for too long. He gasped, tucked a finger under his tie, and loosened it. He turned and walked away from the door, lest Jane Anthony stood on the other side of the peephole studying him.

Ahead, the silver doors of the elevator reflected his image back at him. In the back of his mind, he recalled the high-pitched baby scream from earlier in the evening.

"Nope."

One-Shot pounded down the stairs and into the humid evening.

With another client on the books, One-Shot took the deposit, threw it in the bank, and proceeded to drink away the next week. He considered the deposit "fun money," worthless but for the pleasure it provided, or in this case, the oblivion. If it wasn't for the text from Raven, he would have continued like this until he'd blown it all.

Somehow, the text message from his sister managed to cut through his self-destruction, sober him up long enough to realize he had something else to do.

*Grandpa's ashes are ready.*

With a mouth tasting like he'd been licking a piss-soaked rabbit for the past week, he hopped into the shower, always keeping an eye on the corners. He scrubbed all over, and in the steamy haze of his shower, tried to recall how many days he'd let slip by. *How long has it been since I showered?*

The answers didn't present themselves, and when the shower made his beer too warm, he threw it back, feeling the joy of his Adam's apple jigging up and down in his throat as he polished it off. One loud burp later, he turned off the shower and stepped into the womb-like warmth of the bathroom.

*Grandpa's ashes.* Cold responsibility settled on his shoulders, and he shivered.

After performing his morning rituals, he stepped into his apartment, walking naked among his meager possessions. In the bedroom, he found some clothes that were clean-ish, threw them on, grabbed his keys, and stepped outside. As soon as he left his apartment his anxiety spiked.

*How the fuck do I even get to Oregon?*

*I could fly.* The thought left him feeling queasy in the day's sunlight.

On the street, he passed a man speaking into his cell phone, full Yinzer accent on display. One-Shot didn't speak with the accent, had grown up sounding like everyone else in his family. At times, he wished he had one. Maybe it would make him stand out a little more, though it was handy to be able to blend in anywhere at any time. He lived with that tug-of-war in his soul, of wanting to be left completely alone and wanting to belong in some fashion.

Maybe on the reservation he would fit in like a puzzle piece, find his place, and never want to leave. He doubted it though. He'd fuck it up somehow. That's what he always did. Most people who were fuck-ups didn't know they were. One-Shot had the misfortune of being aware of his nature. Put anything good in his life, and he could mess it up.

*Sadie.*

One-Shot pounded on the side of his head with his balled fist. A woman who walked past him took a wide-arcing berth, and he turned around and yelled, "I'm not crazy!"

She walked faster, and One-Shot shrugged his shoulders, continuing his quest to find his car.

He found it fifteen minutes later, parked in the area he imagined it had. The plastic sheet had been ripped from the busted back window. When he sat inside, he smelled the faint odor of piss. *Did I piss in the car, or did someone else come along and done me the favor?*

Already pressed for time, he started the Accord. As he drove, hot air rushed into his car, somehow augmenting the smell of piss rather than dissipating it. With a sneaky hand, he reached between his legs and checked his own crotch for wetness to see if the smell was coming from him. You knew your drinking was bad when you still worried about drunk things happening to you while you were stone cold sober.

*I gotta stop drinking.*

In no time, he found himself in front of Grandpa's house. When he stepped inside, it was emptier. His mom was there along with Raven. They hugged him, made him feel emotions he didn't want to feel.

His head swam with sadness, and rather than cry like everyone else, he had to fight the urge to punch holes in the walls. His mother was selling the place. That's why it was so empty inside. Gone was the couch, taken to the dump as no one would buy it. Grandpa's bookshelves sat empty, all the books donated to the library the way he would have wanted.

"We thought you might want to dig through his records before we give 'em away," his mom said.

But he didn't. Honestly, he didn't want any remembrances of Grandpa. They would only remind him, make him sad, and goddammit, he was over this already. Because it was his mom, and he wanted to show her the respect she deserved in her time of grieving, he dutifully went into the dining room, squatted down, and leafed through the shelf holding Grandpa's records.

There must have been two hundred, their edges faded white with wear and tear from being slid in and out of the cupboard.

An unbidden memory came to him: his grandfather sitting at the kitchen table, his glass mug glowing gold with beer, bubbles climbing up through the liquid to burst on the surface, and a thick head resting on top like a layer of cake frosting. The record player spun, and some warbly country-music singer wailed away, their pain contagious.

"Paaaaallllllmmmer!" Grandpa bellowed. "Pick me out another record!"

"What do you wanna hear?"

"I don't care."

Arnold, long before he'd become One-Shot, squatted down on the ground, thumbing through the records, shoving the paper bag full of empty beer cans out of the way. He didn't recognize any of the names on the records, knew nothing about any of them, though sometimes he caught a tune he liked in passing. When Grandpa drank, you just stayed out of the way, but when he called to you, it was best to go. For the most part, his grandpa was a happy drunk, liked to sit at the table, listen to his music, and sometimes play solitaire, his thin fingers flipping cards with a casual intensity. Arnold never understood his love for solitaire. Seemed like a loser's game. No skill involved, just pure chance. But that's the way life was, he supposed.

Eventually, Arnold settled on the cover of a record with two smiling white men in ridiculous white hats, the necks of their instruments pointed to the air like mortars. Their eyes stared off-camera, and the entire background had been splashed with an icky mustard color. "The Stanley Brothers" had been stenciled across the front in Kelly green. He slid the record to his grandfather who took it gingerly in his hands, handled it like treasure.

He lifted the arm of the record player, pulled the previous record from the turntable, and slid it back into its sleeve. Like a priest holding a sacred relic, he pulled The Stanley Brothers from the sleeve, perfect midnight vinyl, grooved and loaded. As one might set a child in its crib, he laid the vinyl on the turntable. With a steady hand, he lowered the arm, and country crap blasted over the speakers.

One-Shot never understood how Grandpa could stand that country shit. It was the worst, reminded him of all the hillbilly, camo-wearing fucks out in the sticks who had it in for anyone who wasn't white enough. But his grandpa loved it, and occasionally, when One-Shot managed to suspend his dislike, he would find cold, hollowing songs that did something to his soul. If he had been drinking with his grandfather, this sensation likely would have been amplified, but he hadn't imbibed back then, had sworn off alcohol and vowed never to touch the stuff. You could do shit like that when you were a kid, and it wasn't readily available. *I'll never smoke! I'll never drink! I'll never have sex until I'm ready to marry! I would never drink and drive!* All that bullshit you could crow when you were still wet behind the ears.

His grandpa was drunk, slurring his words a bit. "Lemme tell you something, Palmer, my Palmer, my beautiful Palmer. You hear me?"

Arnold had sat down at the kitchen table as soon as Grandpa had begun to speak. When he called your name, started freestyling it, you knew you were in for some conversation. And Grandpa could talk, was fun to talk to. Not all the time, but most of the time. "I hear you."

"Lemme tell you something, Palmer. Listen to me."

Grandpa's eyes widened behind his thick eyeglasses, and he grew serious, the overt gravitas of one who was about to spill the hidden secrets of the universe, discovered floating in the bottom of a sudsy mug. "Don't you fall in love, my Palmer, my Palmer, my beautiful Palmer."

He remembered wanting to laugh then, wanting to tell his grandpa that so far that hadn't been a problem. As a middle-schooler, he had been little more than a face in the crowd. Making friends had been impossible in his new school. He'd had more fights than conversations with the other students. Sixth grade was a terrible time to move...the worst. All the people in his school had known each other from the time they were in elementary school. There was no room for him, and they liked to remind him of that daily. They did this by throwing shit at him when he wasn't looking and by calling him names behind his back and to his face. No, falling in love had been the least of his concerns back then.

"Love is the end. You're too smart for that, too smart to throw it all away. Don't you fall in love, Palmer. Wait until you're done with college, and then you'll be ready." His grandpa continued his tirade, decrying the lure of love, talking about how it would ruin his life if he let it. Then, things took a turn for the red-faced worst when Grandpa began talking about sex, which Arnold had kind of thought they'd been talking about all along. "If you're gonna have sex, then use a condom."

He'd heard the advice before, but that's not what embarrassed him.

"You don't want a baby. Oh, lord, you do not want a baby. You knock someone up and it's over for you. There goes everything. All your time, your money. All gone." He took a sip from his beer, his gray and black mustache collecting Olympia foam for a moment before he swiped the back of his arm across his face. "If you're gonna do it, then put a rubber on the end of your pecker."

Flecks of spittle landed on Arnold's crossed arms as his grandfather emphasized the word pecker. He thought most people's families wanted them to find love, to find someone who cared about them. Bad enough to be told not to fall in love, but then, Grandpa had to go and talk about his actual penis, which, let's face it…no one wants their family talking about their genitals. In his head, he carried around the embarrassment for the entire week at school, avoiding looking at the girls in his class, lest he fell in love.

Like all good advice, it was easy to follow, until it wasn't easy anymore. He'd fallen in love, done exactly what his grandpa had warned him about all those years ago. Prophetic? Had he gone out and actively waged war against the advice? While One-Shot was a contrarian, he tried not to be a masochist.

No. Like most people his age, he had failed to resist the urge of his own emotions, had succumbed to them, the advice vanishing from his mind as soon as the blood rushed into the nether regions of his body. All thought vanished, replaced by lust. Not a lot of people outside of Buddhist monks can resist that urge. His grandpa must have known.

With a shaky hand, One-Shot reached out and grabbed The Stanley Brothers record from the pile. This one would be alright. This one would fit comfortably in the top shelf of his closet, never to be seen again... Unless he moved out at some point.

With the record in his hand, he returned to his mother, stood next to the urn, listened to her instructions. She spoke in a slur, and he grew nervous she was going to knock over the urn, causing them to have to scoop Grandpa back in with their bare hands.

"Do you want to see him?" his mom asked.

The thought horrified him. Scared him to death really. "What do you mean see him?'

"You can see," his mother said, and then her hands were reaching for the urn.

Raven, busy mixing up a pot of mac and cheese in the kitchen called out to them. "What are you doing?"

"Mom's taking the top off the urn!" he cried.

"Why?"

"I don't know!"

"We should see if he's here," his mother said by way of explanation. "I'd hate to have you go all the way out to Oregon and find the urn empty."

"You didn't look already?" he asked. He wanted to run away, to leave his mother staring at Grandpa's burnt ashes. But if he ran now, he would never come back, and he owed Grandpa. Even though he'd not followed his advice, he should have, knew now all the things his grandpa had told him were true or would come true. Such was the way with wisdom. You could listen to the wise all you wanted, but until you yourself were wise, it was impossible to follow in their path.

Mom popped the top off the urn, and One-Shot flinched, expecting a plume of gray ash to come geysering out. But it didn't. They crowded around the urn and peered inside. The shine of plastic greeted their eyes. Sealed within the plastic was a curry-looking powder, with chunks of bone sprinkled throughout like beach sand peppered with broken shells.

"How do you know it's him?" One-Shot asked.

His mom shrugged. "Guess we just have to take their word for it."

"It creeps me out," Raven said.

"Be nice to Grandpa," Mom retorted. They fell silent then, waiting for Mom to put the lid back on the urn.

"Is this how they used to do it back in the day?" One-Shot asked.

"Do what?" Raven asked.

"Funerals."

Mom laughed then. "Our tribe used to bury them."

"Did they have shovels?" One-Shot asked.

"Fuck if I know," Mom said. It was like that with many things from the past.

Finally, Mom picked up the lid of the urn and tried to replace it. It took a few tries. Whether that was because she was drunk or emotionally spent, One-Shot didn't know. When the lid clicked home, she let out a deep sigh, and One-Shot found he too could breathe easier.

They walked away from Grandpa, leaving him to rest on the kitchen counter.

His mother homed in on the fridge like a wolf taking down wounded prey. She ripped the fridge open, fiddled around in its guts, and came up with a tasty morsel, more blue mountains, more silver aluminum. She popped the top, took a wet sip, and then handed it off to Raven. She always did that. Her little joke on her kids. Once, when Raven had pressed her on the peculiar habit, Mom simply said, "I don't want to give you anything that's not good enough."

She popped the top of another can, took a sip, and handed it to One-Shot. Her hair was gray and thin. It did that when she was stressed, thinned out so you could see her almond-colored scalp. Thoughts of his mother feeling so deeply made him uncomfortable, and he resisted the call of his feet to flee.

He'd be a brave Indian, stoic, emotionless. Together the family sat around the dinner table, the specter of Grandpa visible on the counter.

"You know what to do?" his mom asked.

"Huh?"

"With the ashes, dumb-dumb," Raven said.

One-Shot shot her the finger and took a sip of his beer. When he'd swallowed and given himself enough time to straighten the conversation in his mind, he said, "Uh, go to the grave and put him with Grandma. Does he have a plot or something?"

His mom shook her head.

"Then what the hell am I supposed to do?"

"You're gonna do it the old way. Hands and knees."

One-Shot was tempted to grab his beer and pitch it back in one go. Maybe he was going crazy. Maybe this was all part of it. Perhaps he was hearing everything incorrectly, and the crossed wires in his brain were making him think he had to go to an Indian cemetery, get down on his hands and knees, and dump Grandpa's ashes on his grandmother's grave.

*Yeah, that seems like something a crazy person would do.*

"I just wanna get this right. You want me to go there and dig a hole with my bare hands?"

"You can't walk into a cemetery with a shovel, dumb-dumb." Raven loved calling him that, mostly because he wasn't dumb. Now that Grandpa was dead, he was the smartest person in the family. He guessed it was like calling a big guy Tiny.

"Makes sense."

"Best to do it at night, yeah?" his mother suggested.

Sweat broke out on One-Shot's brow. "Which one of you is going to come bail me out when I get arrested for desecrating an Indian burial ground?"

"They won't do anything," his mom said. "They're too busy running the casino, counting their money."

"What if someone sees me?"

"Run."

His mom and his sister laughed together, their mouths wide open, their cackles echoing in the kitchen.

Raven sipped her beer, walked into the kitchen, and pulled a sheaf of papers off the counter. When she returned, she plopped the papers in front of him and sat down with a groan.

"You shouldn't be drinking with that baby," One-Shot said.

She looked like she wanted to say something, but she held back. Raven grabbed the beer, defiance apparent in her jaw, and threw back a mouthful.

Shaking his head, One-Shot studied the papers in front of him. Directions. He couldn't help but notice the total amount of drive-time. "Forty hours. Jesus." Forty hours on the road, sitting in a single seat, the entire country rushing by. Some people might look at it as an adventure, but not One-Shot. If it hadn't been his grandpa's last wish, he wouldn't even consider making the journey.

"Can I at least borrow one of your cars?" One-Shot asked.

Raven looked out the front window and said, "Fuck no. Have you seen what you do to cars?"

One-Shot took one look at his ride and shrugged his shoulders. Raven had a point. Though his Honda had never been much of a winner, it was definitely in worse shape than when he'd bought it. The sides were dented, the back driver's side window was busted out, and even though Raven didn't know it, the inside smelled like piss and there was no car stereo. On top of that, the heater only had two settings, boiling or completely off. There was no in-between. If you turned the heat on, you also had to roll down the window or you'd be roasted alive.

"I'm just going there and back," One-Shot said.

"There and back is good," Mom said. Her voice sounded different to him. When he turned, she was staring off into the distance, her beer forgotten for the time being, a rarity for Cheye Yeager. "Go in at night. Leave without being seen."

"What are you on about?" One-Shot asked.

His mother blinked, her hands reflexively reaching for her beer. "What?"

"You just got all weird," One-Shot said, turning to Raven for support.

His sister shrugged her shoulders. "How would you know what's weird?"

One-Shot shrugged his shoulders. *I guess I wouldn't.* "Go in at night. Leave without being seen." The words rattled in his head for the rest of the evening as they divvied up the rest of Grandpa's meager possessions, deciding what to keep and what to give away. They wouldn't make money off his things. That was not the way. His things would find new owners, and through them, his grandpa's spirit would live on in the houses of strangers, people who laughed, and drank, and fucked.

When Mother had wound down and dragged herself off to bed, One-Shot caught Raven grabbing another beer out of the fridge. Without stopping to talk to her, he stalked across the yellowed linoleum and pulled the can from her hand.

"What are you doing?" Raven asked, slapping at him, hard. The sound of palm striking face echoed through the house.

"You're pregnant," he said.

Raven smiled at him then. "I'm not."

"What?"

"I had it taken care of."

The beer in his hand weighed a thousand pounds. It dragged his arm down. "Taken care of?"

"Come on, Arnold. Don't be thick."

He held the beer out to her. She snatched it from him and cracked the top, slurped back the piss-colored contents.

"Are you okay?" he asked.

Raven finished drinking. "I think so."

"I'm sorry," One-Shot said.

"What's there to be sorry for?" Raven scoffed. "I mean I could have kept it, but then that dipshit'd be in my life forever. I couldn't handle that." She held the beer low, and when his eyes were drawn to the top of the can, she snaked her hand out and tapped him on the jaw with two fingers, his head flinching to the side. "Besides, you really would make a shit uncle."

"Uh-huh." They fell silent then, mourning the life of the family-member-who-never-was in their own ways.

For One-Shot, his was not the mourning that comes from what could have been, but a reminder of what he'd already given up…with Sadie.

"I gotta go," he said, turning to grab his keys from the hook next to the door.

"I know," Raven answered. "Remember. Go in at night. Leave without being seen."

One-Shot's head snapped around. "What is it with you two?"

"Huh?"

"You just said what Mom said," he accused.

"Okay."

"You don't find that weird? Why do you two want me to go in at night?"

"I don't know what you're talking about. Are you sure you're okay to drive?" Raven studied him as if he was crazy.

"You fuckin' with me?"

"God, you're weird."

One-Shot shrugged. He could have pressed the point some more, but once Raven knew she was getting to you, really hitting your buttons, she wouldn't relent. She'd just keep pounding away at them until you swore at her up and down. No wonder all her relationships failed. Not that his did any better.

He wolfed down the last bite of his burger, flying through the blasted, eastern plains of Wyoming. Roadkill painted the pavement, both fresh and rotting, some little more than flattened mats of fur blowing in the wind. At every turn, he expected to find another herd of rabbits, but if they were out there, they didn't present themselves.

Outside the town of Elk Mountain, the world began to rise. He tilted back, his car, groaning at being forced into such laborious activity.

*Clothes and an oil change. How long since I had the oil changed on this thing?*

The thought fled his mind as he passed a man on the side of the road, his thumb held out for a ride. One-Shot flew past him so fast, the road twisting around a curve, that he didn't have time to study the man's face in his rearview mirror. But the clothes, the hat. *No, it can't be.* But part of him swore it was the same man from the gas station. Brown skin, broad-brimmed hat, that Indian-pattern jacket, faded jeans the color of a pale blue sky.

*No big deal. He just hitched a ride with someone faster than me.*

It made perfect sense, even though it didn't.

*He's lost,* Grandpa said.

"Okay."

Trees sprang up, and the highway closed in on him. For the first time in a thousand miles, he plunged into shadows, the car cooling instantly as he rolled from shadow to shadow up the wrinkled breast of America. The road grew curvier here, winding like a snake between peaks and valleys. If it wasn't for the oncoming traffic, he could feel like he was all alone in the world...which he was, sort of.

*You got me,* Grandpa reminded.

One-Shot shrugged as he slung around a hill, his car not liking the grade of the road as gravity pushed him back against the driver's seat. Up one hill, he had to switch into the left lane to pass a semi that couldn't keep up with the steep angle of the road.

He hoped it wasn't going to be like this the whole way. Then, suddenly, he felt something even worse than the grinding of his car's engine. His stomach fought him, and he knew it was only a matter of minutes before he needed to shit his brains out.

"Fucking Doozy. I shoulda known better than to get a Doozy from Burger Castle."

His stomach gurgled in response, and he gripped the steering wheel tighter, sweat breaking out on his body. Then came the pressure of something angry and violent in his colon.

"Fuck," he muttered. He followed this by releasing an ongoing parade of swears, an obscenity-woven spell to keep the filth in his body trapped inside. Wrapped in the protective aegis of his swear words, he stomped on the gas pedal. He didn't want to think about what he'd have to do if he soiled himself. Drive cross-country naked? Go into a store wearing shitty pants?

*You should have planned better,* Grandpa said.

One-Shot and his Honda Accord became a streaking meteor. The needle on his dashboard read ninety-miles-per-hour for a brief moment before he was forced to slam on his brakes as he squealed around a gentle curve. The world to his left consisted of an ascending tree-covered slope. The world to his right, a field of cleared, green land, rounded and smooth like a scoop of pistachio ice cream, slanting down to a valley floor.

*Gurgle, bubble. Pain.* He flew down the hill, descending into the valley, and there, in the distance, he spotted his salvation. A massive sign, yellow and red, a seashell in the middle.

With his fingers crossed that no cops were painting his car with a radar gun, he accelerated down the hill, the Shell gas station drawing nearer and nearer.

"Oh, fuck," he groaned, pinching his ass cheeks together. His butt had risen off the seat now. To sit at a ninety-degree angle was now a no-go. The pavement rolled on, the garbage bag window bulging out like a prolapsed rectum. He hit the freeway exit ramp at seventy-five-miles-per-hour, squealed across the dry pavement, leaving bits of blackened tire behind like scraps of flesh. He slid to a stop in the parking lot, his arms locked against his steering wheel. Now came the hard part, getting out of the car without squirting his insides all over the place.

He slid out of the Honda with his guts bubbling like a pot of cooking chili. He glanced once at Grandpa, then figured he probably didn't want to come along for this ride. "I'll be back," he said.

Dripping nervous sweat, he clench-walked into the Shell.

"Bathroom?" he yelled at the clerk.

The clerk, sensing his panic, pointed down a hallway, and One-Shot bounced down the hallway on his tippy toes, his butt cheeks vise-tight.

The bathroom wasn't what One-Shot had expected. He had seen one too many horror movies, he guessed. Instead of a dripping, wet mess plastered in graffiti, with glory holes in all the stalls, he found a relatively clean bathroom, as far as gas stations went. He shuffled to the toilet, his hands fumbling at the button of his jeans. Still clenching, he let gravity pull his jeans to the ground.

"Alright, here it goes."

In one swift movement, One-Shot bent and sat on the toilet, thumping down with urgent speed onto the cold porcelain. He relieved himself, bubbling, gurgling and squawking. The relief he felt bordered on orgasmic, and even after he'd voided his insides, he sat on the toilet his body pulsing until it returned to normal.

Goosebumps broke out on his flesh, and he swiped the back of his brown hand across his sweaty forehead.

When he'd finished cleaning up, he vowed then and there to never eat at Burger Castle. *Ninety minutes from entrance to exit? That's quicker than a summer blockbuster.*

As he washed his hands, he tried to avoid looking at the stranger in the bathroom mirror, the memory of his last dalliance with his reflection spinning in the back of his mind.

He awoke Thursday morning, his mouth tasting like he'd chewed on a dirty diaper for the entire evening. With Desby snoring naked on the bed, he stepped into the bathroom, eyed her toothbrush dubiously. In the end, he had to get the taste out of his mouth, so he grabbed her toothbrush and covered it liberally with toothpaste, like he was frosting a cake. When he put the toothpaste back and closed the medicine cabinet door to look at himself in the mirror, he saw something crawling in the corner behind him.

The toothbrush dropped into the sink, clattering. His cock shriveled to nothing, and his balls drew within himself. When he pulled back the shower curtain, there was nothing there, just a wad of Desby's over-processed hair in the drain, no sign of the crawling thing.

"You're fucking losing it, One-Shot." But no, he had seen it. Maybe he wasn't awake yet, maybe he had stumbled into the bathroom half-asleep, stuck with one foot in dream world and one foot in reality. But he'd seen it—a baby, naked and rotting, crawling across the ceiling, watching him from behind, its lips black, its eyes hollow sockets. He left the shower curtain open so the fucking thing couldn't sneak up on him again. Though he was sure it wasn't real, it was better not to leave things to chance.

He fished the toothbrush out of the sink, studied the splat of paste on the brush to see if anything nasty had clung to it. Desby wasn't the tidiest woman around. It was hard to clean when you were hungover all the time. One-Shot knew that from experience. Deciding the toothbrush was good enough, he turned the water on and began brushing his teeth, always keeping an eye on the corner inside the shower, waiting for that freakish baby to poke its head up over the shower curtain.

Around the toothbrush, he said out loud, "You're not crazy."

And maybe he wasn't... Or maybe he was... Probably wouldn't know until it was too late.

When he finished, he went back to bed, threw an arm over Desby and squeezed her breast for a little while until he fell back asleep.

Later that afternoon, One-Shot awoke to the sounds of Desby moving about the apartment. She made a show of cleaning up, putting things away, pulling her panties and bras out of a pile one by one and throwing them in a seldom-used hamper.

She was a broken person with a big heart. Most damaged people were. That's how they got fucked up in the first place. People with tiny hearts could live just fine in this world, motoring through death and misfortune with a shrug and a stiff upper lip. But people like Desby got broken down, treated like shit, and never sought anything better because that way just wound up hurting even more.

One-Shot sat up, groaning from the pounding in his head.

"You wanna do something today?" Desby asked.

"Can't," One-Shot said. "Got a client to meet today."

She nodded, and he sensed the disappointment.

"You wanna do something tomorrow?"

"I don't know why I asked. I get the deal. You're broken. You're all fucked up."

"I'm broken?" he asked, incredulous. *Can she read my mind?*

"Don't give me that shit," she said, using the voice she usually reserved for cutting off drunken assholes at the bar. She'd never used the voice with him though.

"What?"

"I get it, okay—I'm not wife material. But don't treat me like some fucking charity case."

"I'm not."

Her jaw clenched, and he knew a fight was coming. He didn't want anything to do with it, so he stood up, began searching for his clothes.

"I'm getting tired of this, One-Shot."

"Tired of what?" he asked as he pulled on his underwear, already scanning for his jeans.

"You come to my bar, you get all sad, and when you're drunk, you're like the sweetest, gentlest man in the world. In the morning, that man's gone, and all that's left is this...this scared little runaway. That's what you are, One-Shot—a runaway. You run away from everything, but never far enough to be gone for good. When you get lonely or sad, you come crawling right back."

"Enough," he said.

"You're doing it now. Look at you. Soon as I do something other than spread my legs for you, you're running out the door."

*Fuck. She's right.* He sighed, heavy and deep. "Okay. Tell me more."

"That's it!" she shouted.

"Well, what do you want me to do?" *Just fucking tell me and I'll do it. Jesus.*

"I don't know."

He rolled his eyes.

A set of dirty panties smacked him in the face. He sat on the bed like a broken mannequin, heartless inside. Somewhere in his head, there were tears, but he hadn't seen them in some time. He wanted to unleash them, thought maybe they could say more than he could with his words.

"Are you going to say anything?"

"I'm sorry," he managed to say.

She turned her back on him them. "What good is a sorry?"

"It's all I got."

She walked into the small kitchenette, pulled a beer out of the fridge, cracked it open. "Goddammit, One-Shot, you could have so much more."

"I'm happy with what I have."

"And that's the problem, isn't it?"

He followed her into the kitchenette and stood next to her while she looked off into the distance. Fruit flies buzzed in his face from the mess in the sink. He held his hand out, and she handed him the beer. He took a sip, washing away the morning breath that had returned even after he'd brushed his teeth earlier.

He handed it back to her and wrapped his arms around her. "I'll be better."

She laughed then, wounding his pride a bit.

"I will. You'll see. I just got a lot going on right now."

"There's always something going on with you."

"Once I get back from Siletz, we'll figure things out."

She shook her head, obviously didn't believe a word he said. "Can I come with you?" she asked. "I got some vacation time I need to use."

*Fuck. A rock and a hard place.* "This is something I gotta do alone."

"Yeah…? Well, what about me? I'm tired of being alone."

"You're not."

"Get out," she said.

A part of him was relieved, but another part of him felt like a piece of shit. He put the rest of his clothes on and left without saying a word. Nothing he could say then and there would make her happy.

The hard part was he didn't know if he cared. Did he want to make her happy? Did he want to do anything more with her? *Why the fuck do things always have to change?* Raven was pregnant, then she wasn't. Grandpa was dead. Desby wanted more. *Fuck. All I wanna do is live.*

As he stepped from the elevator and left Desby's apartment building, he plunged into the searing sunshine. He hoofed it across town to his apartment, flopped on his couch, and threw his hand over his face. He tried not to think about the world, about how everyone demanded so much of him, but expected so little…and how he often obliged them. Some people were givers; he was a taker, but it hadn't always been that way. Not always. Well, mostly.

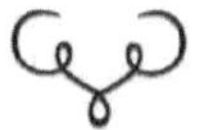

He didn't know how long he had been in the bathroom. The road was timeless.

The man in the mirror across from him was a piece of shit. Even worse, the fucker copied every move he made. But this guy was skinnier than he remembered, had dark circles around his eyes, his hair unkempt and flying every which way. Large pit stains blossomed at the armpits of his t-shirt.

One-Shot flashed the stranger a grin. "You still got it."

The bathroom was out of paper towels, so he wiped his hands on his jeans and prayed he'd gotten the Doozy out of his system in one fell swoop. He certainly didn't want to have to make another stop like that one.

He bought a bottle of water, figured he'd need it after pissing out his insides. Also, it was a sort of penance for the stench he'd embedded in the gas station's bathroom. Outside, he stopped on the sidewalk, cracked open the water, and took a deep sip.

After he finished hydrating, he trudged to his car, opened the door, and flopped inside, the car squealing up and down on its shocks. After fishing his keys from his pocket, he paused, keys dangling mid-air.

*Something's wrong. Something's different.*

He scanned the interior of the car to find what was off. Then he noticed it. The brass urn was missing. Grandpa had gone somewhere.

He hopped out of the vehicle and spun like a girl in a horror movie. Semi-trucks idled in rows, their driver's taking required naps, as smaller vehicles waited by the pumps. A handful of cars filled up the parking spaces in front of the truck stop's convenience store, and he peered inside. Nothing. One-Shot cast his gaze further, beyond the pumps.

There! The bronze gleam of metal caught his eye, and his heart skipped a beat. The urn was in the possession of the

Whistle Man. He had it held up to his ear as if listening to it. Then he turned his head and spoke silent words to the urn, nodding his head the entire time.

One-Shot ran, sprinting across the scorching pavement, narrowly dodging a station wagon pulling into the lot. One-Shot figured the Whistle Man was fucking nuts, so he didn't go in guns blazing. He didn't want to scare the man and have him do something drastic with the urn and the beloved ashes within. Thankfully, the silver duct tape was still in place, but who knew how long until this weirdo ripped the tape off and began stuffing Grandpa's remains in his mouth?

"Hey," he called. "That's my grandpa."

The Whistle Man listened to the urn once more, nodded his head, and held the urn out to One-Shot. He smiled expectantly.

One-Shot gently took it from the man. He spun on his heel, not even wanting to talk to the freak. From behind, he heard foreign words, lots of *k* and *th* sounds. He had no clue what the man was saying.

After waiting for an RV to pass, he crossed the parking lot, slid into his car, and buckled Grandpa into the passenger seat. When he looked up, the Whistle Man waved at him. Through the open window of his car, he could hear the warbling call of the strange man's whistle over the chug of idling engines, the crackle of tires over pavement, and the chiming of gas pumps.

It was then he remembered his gun. Without taking his eyes from the Whistling Man, he slid his hand down into the door pocket, brushed his fingers across the cold metal of the grip. The steel reassured him, made him feel safer, even if it was mostly for show. He started up his car, and it came back to life reluctantly, the entire vehicle shuddering and sighing as it was forced into work once more.

"Not too much longer," One-Shot assured it as he patted the dashboard.

He threw the car into drive and exited the gas station, the Whistle Man waving good-naturedly at him, his lips still pursed as he whistled his haunting little ditty. Even after One-Shot left the man in his dust, he could hear the eerie lilt of the tune.It wasn't until he was on the highway again, alone with his own thoughts and Grandpa that he began to freak out.

"Who the fuck was that guy?" He looked over at Grandpa's urn, waiting for a response, but none was forthcoming.

He rolled through piney hills now, the road twisting and rising and following the path of least resistance. Around him, cars flew by, disappearing into the distance and roaring up on his ass with a frequency that made him feel like his car was stuck on a treadmill. Still amped up over losing Grandpa, he longed just to get to his final destination.

The sun had climbed above his car and began beaming flaming rays of sunshine down on his vehicle. His car lacked power, and as he climbed the eastern breast of the Rockies, he had to turn off the air-conditioner every time he began a steep ascent. Up and up he went, the heat collecting in his car despite the rushing air coming in through all the windows.

His Dr. Pepper grew warm, and sweat began to collect in his arm pits and back. The hair on the back of his head grew wet with perspiration, and he drank his warm Dr. Pepper just to keep hydrated. He wished he'd bought more water as the sticky, sweet drink no longer satisfied him.

At the peak of a hill, he'd click on the A/C as he cruised down the decline. His car seemed to shiver as the air conditioner's compressor clicked on, and One-Shot gasped as the cold air washed over him. He rolled up his windows to take advantage of it, even if it was only for a moment.

In this way, he traveled throughout the day, keeping his eyes peeled for the Whistle Man. Though he had no proof, he sensed the man's evil intentions. He felt as if he was being stalked across the country by the strange fellow.

*What the hell did he want with Grandpa, anyway?*

With every twist in the road, he expected to see him standing there. Though he was fast becoming exhausted, One-Shot couldn't stop. If he did, the Whistle Man would gain on him, find him sleeping on the side of the road somewhere. And then what? What would the Whistle Man do when he found him?

He didn't want to find out, so he kept going, kept pushing himself. The world took on muted shades, and all the cars around him, loaded down with children and coolers and barking dogs, took on sinister tones. The gap-toothed kid smiling at him from the back of a station wagon seemed to mock him, smiling because she knew what the Whistle Man had in store for him.

That dog barking as the car passed him… It was no ordinary dog. It was a devil dog, straight from the pit of Hell, and it was trying to tell him the Whistle Man was coming for him.

One-Shot couldn't resist the urge to glance at every car that passed. He needed to see if the Whistle Man was in there, his lips pursed, whistling his jaunty tune, his silver-black hair spilling from underneath his broad-brimmed hat.

This was how he passed the hours.

As he came down out of the mountains, a valley opened before him, the ground rocky and dotted with scrub foliage. Red rocks rose out of the earth like wads of Play-Doh forgotten in the sun by some giant child. The road twisted less and less, and the traffic grew more frequent. On the edge of Salt Lake City, he thought once more about pulling over and getting some rest.

*In a city as big as Salt Lake City, there's no way the Whistle Man can find me. I hope.*

As he clicked his turn signal on, he prepared to take an exit into the city. Then he saw him, standing on the side of the road, underneath a sign that read "Welcome to Salt Lake City." A crow sat on the Whistle Man's shoulder. The knife of his whistling, though it shouldn't have been audible, infiltrated One-Shot's car, set the fillings in his teeth to vibrating. At the last second, One-Shot swerved back onto the highway, cutting off an SUV. He waved his hand in the air in apology and hurtled onward, through the sprawling city next to the Great Salt Lake. He had no time for it, didn't want the Whistle Man getting his hands on Grandpa again. Or on him for that matter, though in truth, he was mostly worried for Grandpa.

He turned his car north, leaving I-80 behind. This new road, I-84, would take him as far as Portland. Between here and there, thirteen hours of driving. Thirteen hours of solid yellow and white lines hurtling past. Of trees waving futilely at One-Shot, begging him to pull over and spend an evening under their boughs.

But One-Shot wouldn't stop. Not as long as he knew the Whistle Man was out there, his brown hands greedy to hold Grandpa. Onward he rolled, driving north, only to discover the entire left side of his body radiated warmth from a sunburn he wasn't even aware of having collected. His arm and cheek felt like they had been baked.

Scowling, he grew anxious for his journey to end.

Twilight fell, and something strange began to happen. A music filled the car, jangling and eerie. It was a song, but not one he recognized. In the purple light of the day's death, he tried to hear it better, strained his ears as his car ate up concrete miles.

*What the fuck is this song?*

He opened his mouth to talk to Grandpa and…the song grew louder.

*What the fuck?*

His eyes, which felt like they'd been scraped with thirty-grit sandpaper, bugged out of his head as he tested his theory, opening and closing his mouth. The song faded when his mouth was closed. When he opened it, the song grew louder, a jangly, country tune that sounded like something Grandpa would have enjoyed.

His mind, running on sugar and nicotine, had no problem with this latest development. It was clear the aliens who had infiltrated his brain were doing some sort of test on him. That was the only logical explanation. How could he make up a song like this with no musical talent, complete with redneck lyrics and…was that…yeak, a fucking banjo and a washboard in the background?

Anyone who drove past him must have thought he was crazy as he opened and closed his jaw, dug in his ear with his finger, and generally ignored the lines on the road. Then again, maybe they were in on it. In fact, the purpling sky was unlike any he had ever seen in Pittsburgh. Underneath the blue and purple tones, there was a faint tinge of green.

*Perhaps it's in one of the clouds. Yeah, that's it. The flying saucer is hiding in one of those fucking clouds.*

One-Shot stuck a finger out the window, waved it at the sky. "Fuck you, aliens!"

A car rolled by, speeding up an incline, and the old man in the passenger seat looked at him and shook his head. Aliens didn't like profanity apparently.

Undeterred by the interference of aliens in his sacred road trip, One-Shot opened his mouth wide so the aliens' music would blast through his fillings.

"You like this song, Grandpa?" he asked as the sun finally went down, and the sky settled into an onyx mantle.

*It's alright,* Grandpa said.

"Where the fuck have you been?" One-Shot screamed. Grandpa was used to it. One-Shot had graduated into the land of profanity as a teenager and never looked back. To his credit, Grandpa never corrected him. It's not like Grandpa didn't swear all the time; he was no saint.

*I was sleeping. It's easy to sleep in the day. Hard to wake up.*

"Is that because you're dead?"

*What? I'm dead?*

One-Shot's mouth fell open. *How the hell am I supposed to tell Grandpa…*

Grandpa's hoarse, tobacco laugh echoed in the car. The garbage bag window billowed outward, as if catching the laughter.

"Fuck you," One-Shot said. He glanced at the odometer. "And what's with that whistling weirdo?"

*He's lost.*

"Doesn't seem lost. Seems like he's following me across the country.

*That's because he is.*

"Why?"

*He doesn't know the way. Died a long time ago. Far from here. He's been waiting for someone to guide him back.*

"Why doesn't he ask for a ride like a regular human being?"

*Being dead is hard, and he speaks the old language. Doesn't know our ways.*

"Is he a ghost?"

*Not like you think.*

"How is he different?"

Grandpa fell silent.

Onward he drove. He lit himself some medicine, tried to shake off the aliens' brain waves with curative smoke. The cloud of smoke swirled in the air, and through the veil of his own manmade haze, he thought he could see the faint impression of something in the sky.

It moved and hovered at the same time.

"Goddamn aliens are fucking with me."

The alien song blasted on repeat, jangling, warbly, the words just out of reach of his consciousness. The aliens were probably laughing in their ships, their big old heads and midnight eyes crinkling as they chuckled at his plight.

*You need to sleep.*

"I'll sleep when I'm dead."

*Only during the day. At night, you'll be stuck in a jar sealed with duct tape.*

"Don't worry. I'm going to bury you with Grandma."

*Don't go back there.*

"Why not? Why don't you want me to go back?"

*We left for a reason.*

"Tell me," One-Shot demanded. "I'm sick of all this sneaky-sneaky bullshit."

*I won't tell.*

"Well, then I'm going."

*You shouldn't.*

"And I'm bringing whistle lips with me."

*He'll like that.*

One-Shot shook his head. He was tired of the mystery, of the unspoken things in his life. Don't talk about the craziness of your family. Don't talk about the suicides. Don't talk about the reason Grandpa left the reservation. Don't talk about Grandpa's job. Don't talk about the kid Sadie had aborted.

His thoughts stuttered, his rage at aliens forgotten as his heart seized for a moment, and the specter of a tear held at the corner of his eye.

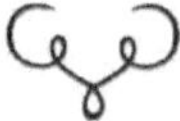

He was almost ready to abandon his plan when a dude in a jogging suit burst through the door. The jogger exited so fast that he startled One-Shot, causing him to bobble Grandpa and almost drop him to the ground. With one hand cradling the urn, he snaked the other arm out and wrapped his fingertips under the flat handle of the door. Pulling, careful not to lose his grip, One-Shot stepped inside the building's lobby.

He remembered the place, every bit of it. The unsightly brass mailboxes with diamond-shaped bits cut out, as if the mail needed to breathe, hung off to the left. The doorman's desk sat occupied by Art, the plumpest doorman you'd ever seen. The carpet rasped under One-Shot's shoes as he walked quickly to the elevator, holding the urn up to hide his face.

Art reclined, his bulbous belly covered by the bottom half of the day's newspaper. When he spotted One-Shot, he sat up and said, "Hey! I know you!"

One-Shot pounded on the button. It lit up, nice and orange like Halloween.

"You can't be in here!"

One-Shot pretended he didn't hear the man. He resisted the urge to press the button once more. Once was always enough for One-Shot.

Art's chair squeaked in relief as he leaned forward and placed his feet on the floor. "Get out of here, you!" Art called.

But One-Shot did no such thing.

As Art rounded the desk, the elevator doors slid open, and One-Shot slithered inside. He pressed the "door close" button once, followed by the button for the seventh floor. Art pounded across the lobby, and One-Shot smiled as the doors slid shut in the doorman's face. He liked Art. He was only doing his job, and even though he'd kicked One-Shot out of the building multiple times, he'd always been pleasant about it. He was a good dude.

The elevator ascended with the typical slowness of a thirty-year-old piece of equipment. At any moment, the cable above could snap and send him plunging to his death. He wondered if he'd wind up covered in Grandpa's ashes if that happened.

"Not today. Right, Grandpa?"

Grandpa didn't answer.

The doors slid open, and One-Shot pounded on the "Emergency Stop" button. He hated to do it to Art, but he needed the time. Sadie's building only had one elevator. In a couple of minutes, Art would notice the elevator wasn't returning, and then he'd have to huff it up the stairs, which would give One-Shot the time he needed. He just hoped Art didn't have a heart attack in the process. The dude was seriously out of shape.

He stalked down the hallway looking for Apartment 708. No one else appeared in the hallway, despite the annoying buzzing emanating from the elevator. Pittsburgh was good like that. People minded their own damn business.

With the urn tucked under his arm like a football, he rapped on the door with his knuckles. *Was that too hard? Too desperate?* He didn't know, just stood back, waiting with his head down.

With each beat of his heart, he imagined Art pounding up the stairs like some sort of Olympian. In his anxious mind, Art became the gold medalist of stair-climbing. Up and up, he went, bounding from one flight of steps to the next, weightless. Once he started really going, he'd rip off his shirt and expose a set of hidden wings covered in white duck feathers, and he'd literally fly up the stairs, bursting forth into the hall.

He became so sure of it that he was staring down the hallway when Sadie opened the door.

"What do you want?"

He turned to look at her. Her jaw was set, her skin sallow, as if she had spent the majority of her life sick and lying in bed. Dark circles ringed her eyes, and he realized how late it was…kind of. After midnight, for sure. Maybe one.

"What is it?" she asked, her patience thin.

"I wanted to see you."

Sadie nodded her head, and it cocked to the side as if to say, "This shit again. I thought I was done with this." She stepped back, pulled her arm around, and placed it on the interior door handle, in preparation for the final insult. Sadie looked up, ready to hit him with another barb, another soul-crushing jape, but the burn never came. "What is that?" she asked, pointing at the urn under his arm.

"It's Grandpa."

Her frosty exterior melted, and her head-tilt adjusted slightly, becoming more of a sympathetic cant. Her clenched jaw relaxed, allowing a thin amount of space between her molars. "Oh, Arnold. I'm sorry."

"No. No. It's okay," he stammered.

"Is it?"

He nodded, though he felt something weird in the corner of his eyes. He decided to change the subject. "Listen. I have to go out to Oregon to spread my grandfather's ashes, and I wondered if you might, you know…want to come along."

"I can't, Arnold. You know that."

He nodded, hating that he was the cause of his own misery. It had been too long since he'd seen her or talked to her. He'd stayed away from her, thinking if he couldn't see her, she might disappear from his mind altogether. He felt like an asshole, an actual sphincter, behind which rested so much shit the little knot of wrinkled flesh couldn't hope to open wide enough to excrete everything he needed to. So much to say, not enough hole to say it. Was that a saying? If not, it should be.

"I'm sorry."

"I know," she said back.

"Well…aren't you sorry?" he asked. In his head, he had imagined that over time without him, she would come to see the error of her ways. Would realize she had done him wrong.

"No, Arnold. It was the right call."

"How can you say that?" he asked. "We could have been something."

"Good night, Arnold." She was sad now. He'd done it to her again. It seemed every interaction he'd had with Sadie had ended the same way since the abortion.

He leaned forward, ready to stop the door with his foot.

"Stop!" a gasping voice yelled.

He turned to see Art standing there, his hands on his thighs, sweat running down his cheeks.

"You *are* an Olympian," One-Shot said in awe as Sadie shut the door in his face. He looked at the door for half a beat, realized he'd probably fucked things up even more. Then he turned and faced Art.

The doorman straightened his back and plodded in One-Shot's direction. "'I'm gonna kick your ass, Arnold."

"You gotta catch me first," One-Shot howled as he took off running. He was glad Sadie's apartment building had two stairwells. Though he might not look it, Art was a tough customer. If he got his hands on you, he'd manhandle you right out the front door. One-Shot knew from personal experience.

Six flights later, One-Shot lowered his shoulder and slammed through the stairwell door. He pounded across the lobby into the humid night air. He ran for his car, shooing away a homeless dude who had gotten too close to it. "Don't piss in there!" One-Shot yelled.

"I'm not an animal, you fucker," the man growled, backing away.

"Fuck you, Arnold!" a voice yelled behind him.

As One-Shot threw open the car door, he turned to find Art flipping him the bird. "Sorry, Art!"

"Fuck you!"

One-Shot waved once to show there were no hard feelings, and then he plopped down into the vehicle. He fished Raven's directions off the passenger seat, took a cursory glance at them, and then started his car.

As he passed Art standing on the sidewalk, the man hocked a loogey on the passenger-side window.

"Really?" One-Shot called.

In his rearview mirror, Art waved his middle finger at him. One-Shot took the next right to erase the image, and then he was on his way to Oregon, somewhere to the west.

His mouth opened, and the jangly song came back full force, channeling through his molars. Don't talk about Sadie. Don't talk about the kid. *Boy or girl?* He didn't know. It was too soon. He swam through his thoughts, a swimming pool full of razor blades. Each stroke brought him more pain.

*You fell in love,* Grandpa said.

"I did."

*I told you not to.*

"I couldn't control it."

*I know. I just hoped.*

The alien song made his teeth rattle in his skull, and he chomped down on his tongue to keep from screaming. His eyes dialed in on the road. The letters on the signs began to swim, and a bubble of rage burst in his chest.

"You're gonna fuck with the signs now? You fucking intergalactic pieces of shit!" He shoved his fist out the window, waved it defiantly at the aliens hiding in their cloud fortress. "You sick fucks! You fucking sick fucks!"

*You tell 'em,* Grandpa said.

He continued telling them for a good three miles. The cars behind him, freaked out by his behavior and One-Shot's swerving, sped by, passengers gawking at him with terrified, round eyes. *Perhaps they were the alien ground crew, wondering how much further they could push him.*

Then they did it, the ultimate test. They started laying babies in the middle of the road.

The first one took him by surprise. Nestled in a blue onesie, it reared up out of the night, its tiny arms waving in the air, its covered feet punching at the sky. He barely missed it, swerved into the next lane, and cursed the aliens some more.

*It's not real,* Grandpa said.

But One-Shot wasn't hearing that noise. All well and good for a dead man in an urn to say the baby in the road wasn't real, but he wasn't the one driving the car. Grandpa wouldn't have to live with the consequences if he was wrong.

Ahead, he caught another flash in the road, this one bubblegum pink. He swerved once more, came close to colliding with a passing car. The man in the car flipped him off like a genuine human being, and One-Shot apologized, though the man had no chance of seeing or hearing him.

One-Shot glued his eyes to the road as the babies appeared with more frequency. His tires squealed as he swerved left and right, dodging the fleshy obstacles the aliens had left in the road.

A part of him knew he was freaking out, that he was having some sort of psychotic break, but then again…what if he wasn't? What if those onesied babies were real, and he plowed right over them? He couldn't live with himself if that were the case. If he hit one of those wriggling bundles of joy with his car and felt the tires roll over their fragile bodies, he would reach into the pocket of his door, pull his gun out, and make things right. But he didn't want to do that, so he slowed down, swerving as the aliens placed their sick traps in the road.

Cars flew past, blasting their horns and gesturing at him to get off the road. He wanted to…wanted to escape the highway, find someplace to sleep. But he knew he was safe in his car, safe if he kept moving. They couldn't just lift his car into the air with a tractor beam. It'd probably show up on radar at that point, and then the air force would get involved, shoot the gray fuckers right out of the sky.

Traveling at thirty miles-per-hour, One-Shot wasn't prepared for the escalation of the situation. The next round of road babies made his heart drop. They were lined up across the pavement…fifteen of them laying head to toe. He was so surprised by the sight he lost a half-second of reaction time, a half-second that would cost him.

He jerked the wheel to the right, sending his car swerving sharply toward the shoulder. His right wheel dropped off the edge of the road, and his car bounced violently as he slammed on the brakes and wound up shooting across the freeway. His car was out of control, and he struggled with the wheel as his vehicle began fishtailing back and forth across the highway. Eventually, he drove off the pavement, bouncing into a ditch, the bottom of his car slamming off the turf at the side of the road.

As his car came to a stop, he gripped the steering wheel, tried to search through his memory of what had just happened, tried to figure out if the violent bouncing of his vehicle had been due to his tires going off the road or because... Because he'd run over a baby. He placed his arm on the headrest of the passenger seat, craned his neck around to see if he could see any lumps or blood smears in the road. Seeing nothing, he turned back around and swiped the sweat off his forehead.

The car's engine ran, angry and off-kilter, and One-Shot let his foot off the brake, turned the wheel, and waited for a semi-truck to pass before he got back on the road. He wondered what the semi-truck driver made of all the babies in the road.

*They're not there,* Grandpa said.

One-Shot knew this to be true and untrue at the same time. They were there, in some way, or he wouldn't have been able to see them.

As he pulled onto the road, he felt the car shift and drag across the pavement, pulling to the right. *A flat.* Though the smart thing to do would have been to pull over then and there, One-Shot had to get away from the scene of the crime, if one had indeed been committed. Although, if the cops pulled him over, he would just tell them the aliens had put them there.

*Yeah, that's it. It's the aliens' fault.*

Two slow miles down the road, One-Shot pulled off to the shoulder with his hazards flashing. His car sighed as he killed the engine.

Outside, the night air still held the warmth of day. A semi-truck rushed by, buffeting One-Shot with warm air, then all fell silent on his side of the highway.

As he shoved the key into the lock of his trunk, a field bounded by rusty barbed wire spread off into dark infinity. To his left, the specter of rushing headlights glowed on the underside of trees lining the top of the berm that separated the eastbound traffic from the west.

Inside his trunk, he ripped up the stained carpet, pulled out his spare tire and the stupid miniature jack that seemed to come with all cars these days. He tossed his spare onto the ground like a corpse. It bounced with a clang. He walked around to the driver's side and set the emergency brake.

As he walked around to the flat tire on the front passenger's side, he took note of the stillness of the highway. It didn't seem natural. Cars should be flying by. It wasn't that late yet, was it? He would have stopped and waited to see if more cars would come along, but there was that whole "maybe I just ran over a baby" thing.

After stomping the lug nuts loose on his car, he placed the jack down and began the slow, laborious process of lifting his car. Around and around he went, his knuckles scraping the pavement the first ten half-turns.

*Always buy your own jack,* Grandpa howled from the passenger seat.

"Easy for you to say."

*I know.*

Once the vehicle was high enough, he undid the lug nuts, storing them in the pockets of his jeans, except for one which fell to the pavement and rolled underneath the car. One-Shot ripped the tire off and threw it on the ground. He picked his spare up, his own body seeming to strobe in the flash of his car's hazard lights. One-Shot didn't know why, but he gave the spare tire a good bounce on the ground. He supposed he'd seen someone in movies do the same thing once. It almost bounced away from him, and he cursed himself for doing movie shit.

Squatting down, he placed the tire on the wheel studs, then tried to hold it steady with one hand while he fished in his pocket with the other.

From the field at his back, something rustled. The sound startled him, causing him to drop the lug nut he'd fished out of his pocket. Forgetting about the tire a moment, he worried a bear or a bobcat or whatever the fuck lived out here was sneaking up on him (*a herd of bunnies*). He spun and peered into the darkness, looking for a set of eyes glowing with each flash of his hazard lights.

"Who's there?" he called, though he didn't know if he would prefer a response or not. No one answered. Instead, more rustling, only now it seemed to be coming from multiple spots.

"Fuck this," One-Shot said, then he fished another lug nut out of his pocket and tried to attach it to the wheel stud as fast as he could. As with most things, he fucked it up a few times before he could get it on straight.

Behind him, the rustling neared, and underneath the rustling, something even worse—the struggling breath of something exerting itself, a small echoing grunt between breaths.

*Get the wheel on,* Grandpa called.

"What the fuck do you think I'm doing?"

He placed another lug nut into place. Behind him, the tall grass shifted in the shadows.

Swear words filled his mind, and his fingers, numbed by fear, had a difficult time placing the third lug nut in place. The threads finally caught, as gurgling sounds erupted from the grass. The sound disturbed him more than it should have. He couldn't say why.

He stood up and spun. "Goddammit, who the fuck is out there?" He reached into his pocket, pulled out his cell phone, turned on the flashlight, and peered into the waving grasses. "If you don't come out of there, I'm gonna fuck you up."

A small cry came from the grass—not that of an adult cry but of a baby. One-Shot's stomach dropped down to his balls, and the moisture evaporated from his mouth. With his flashlight in one hand and fear hammering his body, he fumbled for the last lug nut in his pocket, placed it on the wheel stud.

As he spun it home, another noise hit his ears. A sharp noise, the product of wind rushing over wet lips. The lilting whistle jolted him like a cattle prod. He spun the fourth lug nut home, tightening it as much as he could with his fingers.

He felt on the ground for the fifth lug nut, the one that had rolled under the car. His hands scraped against the dry pavement, still warm from the sun's assault. The whistling grew louder as the crying intensified.

Behind him, the sound of something rattling against the barbed-wire fence made him almost shit himself. He aimed his flashlight at the fence. The sounds were close now. He was on the verge of running down the road and abandoning his car. As the flashlight of his cell phone splashed across the barbed wire fence, he beheld a sickening sight. Lumpen babies, their flesh a dead white, pressed against the fence, their soft skin splitting under the jagged tips of the barbs. But they didn't stop. Their limbs stunted and short, pulled and struggled with the fence, blood coursing from their wounds.

He couldn't take his eyes from them, even though he didn't want to look anymore. Eyes glued to the nightmare before him, One-Shot pawed underneath the car, feeling around for the final lug nut.

As the babies tried to press their flesh through the fence, their crying rocked his eardrums, made him want to jab his fingers in his ears, but both his hands were occupied. As his hand scraped along the pavement underneath his vehicle, he realized something. The whistling had stopped. At the same time as this dawned on him, something brushed against his fingertips, grabbed him by the wrist. He screamed as whatever it was twisted his arm, turned his hand palm side up. And then he felt something cold and heavy drop into his hand—the last lug nut.

The word "fuck" fell from his mouth as a mantra, a magical shield to protect him from the horrors of the night. With trembling hands, he placed the last lug nut on the wheel stud, waiting for the creature underneath the car to pull him under and do whatever strange whistling men did to living people when they caught them.

He spun the lug nut tight enough for a few miles at least. He left the jack and the spare tire where they were, too frightened to bother packing them up. The babies wailed their complaints as he plopped into the driver's seat, the small lug wrench gripped in his hand. Fear punched him, knocked the wind out of him, and he spun to look in the back seat, only to be greeted by the sight of empty Dr. Pepper cans, fast food bags, and junk food wrappers.

With the Whistle Man nowhere in sight, he turned the key in the ignition and floored it. The jack fell over on its side and clanged against the bottom of his car. He cut the wheel to the left and swerved away from it, leaving his flat tire lying in the road.

He wiped the sweat from his face with a tremulous hand. He worried his tire would come flying off at any moment. Two miles up the road, he pulled off to the side and tightened the lug nuts, the entire time waiting for the Whistle Man to appear or for dead babies to come crawling after him. But nothing happened, just the roar of passing vehicles and his own frantic breathing. He began to wonder if he had imagined the whole thing, would have preferred it actually. When the lug nuts were as tight as possible, he threw the lug wrench in the backseat and plopped into the car, feeling a little calmer, a little saner.

*I've been up too long That's all.* Whether this was true or not didn't matter to One-Shot. If it wasn't true, and the Whistle Man and the dead babies were real, what the fuck could he do about it? He was in the middle of nowhere with only his dead grandpa's ashes for company. Stopping now wasn't an option.

If it was all in his mind, then he had nothing to worry about in the first place. Either way, he couldn't stop.

*You don't have to go,* Grandpa said.

But One-Shot didn't listen. He hadn't driven thirty-five hours straight across the country just to turn back now. Besides, he didn't want to think about home. His job, his family, Sadie, all these things became less important the further away he drove. Perhaps he'd find a new life in Siletz, a place where he could settle down and do nothing, not even think.

Maybe he could get a house on the reservation, sit on the porch and watch the world go by. Wouldn't that be nice? Instead of always worrying about money, about bills, about having to go out and earn a living, he could get himself a rocking chair, sit on the porch, drink a beer every now and then as he watched the seasons change.

Through the entirety of Idaho, which was only a few hours' drive, he fantasized about it, thought about giving up everything and starting over, a blank slate, *tabula rasa.*

*You'd miss them all,* Grandpa said.

"Yeah, so? Life is missing people."

*You don't believe that.*

"I don't know what I believe."

*You will learn it soon enough. Turn around, my dear. Head back home where you belong, Palmer.*

"How do you know I don't belong in Siletz?"

*I left for a reason.*

"What reason?"

*They wanted your uncle.*

"Uncle Harry? Why would they want him?"

As he asked the question, a ray of sunshine rose behind him, and Grandpa's voice faded away before he could make out the words. The sun clawed its way into the day, a giant orange ball reflected in the rearview mirror.

He was in Oregon now. The hills sloped downward on the western slope of the Rockies, leading to desert hills. Grandpa slept now, slumbered silently in his urn. One-Shot hoped it was large enough, hoped he was comfortable all snuggled up in its metal depths. It had cost hundreds of dollars and was a poor substitute for a house, but he hoped Grandpa was cozy.

The world came alive in plum-orange glory, and as the morning wind swept through his vehicle, he knew he was getting closer. Orange gave way to blue, and the road lit up as the sands of Oregon's hilly eastern desert reflected the sun back at him. Eventually, a river appeared, springing up deep and blue to his right as he plowed westward. He stopped to refuel at a gas station in a desert town, stood in the early morning desert heat, swiping the sweat off his brow.

He existed outside of society now, stood stinking and filthy, leaning against his car while everyone else went about the business of living. He looked longingly at the trunk of his vehicle, thought of climbing inside and curling up, baking forever in the trunk of his Accord. "Could be nice," he said to himself. A woman in jeans eyed him as if One-Shot was the crazy one, as if she was sane for spending one-third of her life doing work for someone else's table scraps, as if she had it all together because she had a mortgage and more bills than she could ever pay off.

"Room for two," he said to her, chuckling a raspy tobacco laugh.

She hurried on, and he coughed and spat a wad of phlegm on the ground. It glistened back at him in the sunshine. A wind kicked up from the west, spinning a cloud of dust in circles in the distance. When his tank was full, he hopped inside and continued his journey, carving through Oregon like a surgeon's scalpel, leaving a raw wake of weirdness in his tracks.

The Oregon desert gave way to lush mountainsides. The river, older than anything in the land, had carved deep and hard for millions of years, leaving behind a mess of crags and hills that towered above One-Shot as he cruised along I-84. Pine trees, persistent and unconcerned with growing on crooked ledges, jutted up all around as he twisted his way through the outskirts of Portland.

He was glad to see color again. Greens, deep and vibrant, greeted him wherever he turned. The desert air had vanished, and he was amazed at how quick the transition had been. One minute he was surrounded by desolation, passing abandoned shanty villages where people had tried to eke out a living, and the next, he was cruising through an evergreen jungle, traveling on the back of a great paved worm winding its way along the riverbank.

Cars flew by him, and his stinging eyes would barely stay open. In order to stay awake, he chain-smoked, filling his car with tobacco smoke. His throat hurt now, felt dry as the desert he'd left behind. The Dr. Pepper no longer offered the soothing properties it once had. He'd smoked too much. The lines on the road, deep yellow and bright white, locked him into position, and he plowed onward, guided by a foot that seemed disconnected from his body. He had no idea how the impulses from his brain could make it through the block of pain in his lower back all the way down to his foot. He sat up, and his spine cracked angrily.

"100 miles to Portland," a sign read. The stack of directions sat in the passenger seat. He'd consulted them briefly at the beginning of his journey, but in the end, all he'd had to do was keep heading west. Follow the signs west, and you'll get there, *Manifest Destiny* or some such shit.

Somewhere along the way, he'd have to turn south…but just where was a mystery to him. Cruising along the highway, he tried to multitask, to read his sister's directions and steer at the same time. The printed words swam in front of his stinging eyes, the letters taking on a life of their own. He alternated between looking down to decipher the words and preventing himself from driving off into the river. During one of these transitions, he lifted his head and spotted the man standing on the side of the road, dancing in his black hat, twirling in circles, the eerie whistle of his pursed lips somehow reaching One-Shot's ears at sixty-miles-per-hour.

He flew past him, failed to make eye contact with the man, and then craned his neck to see him in his rearview mirror. He was so intent on seeing the man, he didn't realize he was drifting out of his lane, right into the path of a semi-truck. It blared its horn at him, and his heart did a jig in his chest. Panic-stricken, he swerved back into his own lane, his tires squealing on the pavement.

With a quick shot of adrenaline rushing through his system, he experienced a solitary moment of clarity. He wasn't going to make it to the coast if he kept going. He needed to stop somewhere, sleep a little bit. The hard part was done. He needed oblivion—to rest his aching brain, his aching back, his aching backside.

"Portland. Once I get to Portland, I'll take a nap."

The green world flew by, a blur of towering trees, their limbs stretching to the sky. The concrete ribbon of the highway flowed onward, and One-Shot with it. He allowed himself a moment to soak it all in, to really appreciate the beauty of the world around him, and it *was* beautiful, with the sun shining down from above, the birds of prey whirling in the sky, the faint ripple of whitecaps on the river's agitated blue surface. The view almost made him wish he had someone to share it with.

Grandpa yawned, as if just waking up. *You did have someone to share it with,* he said sleepily. Then Grandpa went back to sleep. It was too hard to be awake in the day, One-Shot supposed.

"I did have someone. Could have had two someone's, you know what I mean?"

Just like that, the beautiful vista vanished, and he was back in the lobby of the Planned Parenthood, waiting for Sadie to reappear, lighter in some way, and heavier at the same time. All around, people sat, their faces hanging off their skulls. They sat as if they were in church, nary a smile among the lot.

In most waiting rooms, people made small talk, discussed their day, and the inconsequential minutiae of their futures. But not here, not in this waiting room.

In here, they sat like statues, here to do a hushed, whispered thing that would stick with them the rest of their lives. One-Shot had tried to talk Sadie out of it, said he would raise the kid on his own if he needed to. But Sadie didn't want it and said he was too irresponsible. A bartender couldn't be a dad. And then he'd thought of all the bartenders he'd known, and goddammit, she was right. Oh, some of them had kids, but they were as much a part of their lives as One-Shot's own father was a part of his.

"I'll go back to school," One-Shot had pleaded. "I'll become a lawyer."

Sadie had shaken her head then, put her soft hand on the side of his face, even as the tears gleamed in her eyes. "I don't want it."

And he had to accept it, because she was the mother and that was the way it was. He tried to be good about it, but in the waiting room, he had to fight the urge to go bursting into the operating room or whatever the fuck they had back there and drag Sadie out. But it was her choice, and she'd made it.

He tried to forgive her for making the decision. It must have been a hard one to make. She didn't do it with joy in her heart. One-Shot didn't blame her. He knew he was something of a deadbeat, a low-ambition vagabond content with doing just enough work to keep a roof over his head, food in his belly, and alcohol in his gut. He wasn't a good guy; he was just a guy.

No, he didn't blame her; he blamed himself. Knew if he had taken life seriously, she might have wanted to keep the baby.

"What the fuck!" One-Shot yelled.

On the side of the road, he spotted the Whistle Man standing there, his thumb out, smiling, his black hat pulled down to cover his eyes. As he neared the hitchhiker, the man lifted his head and winked at him.

His heart thundered like a drum.

After that, One-Shot's fear grew, irrational and massive. He forgot about the moment when Sadie had emerged. He forgot about the nights he lay next to her, wondering if they would ever return to what they had been before. He forgot about the moment he had left her key on the coffee table and walked out to live on his own, just a scrap of a letter sitting on the table as explanation, not even well-written.

How could he think about all that stuff when that fucking magic Indian kept appearing on the side of the road? The nearer he got to Portland, as the river and the countryside gave way to urban sprawl and homeless camps, blue tarps and refuse, the more he spotted the Whistle Man, peeking around trees, lifting the flaps of shanty-town tents and peeking out at him. He was like a goddamn, brown-skinned Waldo, and One-Shot had a knack for finding him.

Once, he thought he spotted a mural of the man painted on the backside of an abandoned building as he wound his way through town. Yawning, his sanity on the edge of vanishing forever, One-Shot took an exit on the far side of Portland, spun and twirled his way around rough looking road, between concrete barriers plastered with all sorts of colorful graffiti.

He tried to remember how to get back to where he was. In his mind and on the highway, he tried to stencil the coordinates to sanity on his soul while also memorizing where the highway exit had dumped him out. He drove until he found a Safeway parking lot, and then he parked. One-Shot reclined his car seat as far as it would go, and his back thanked him. His legs, too long to straighten out, did no such thing. In his reclining position, he tried to fall asleep, but the sounds of the city were too many.

One man, seemingly out of his mind or whacked out on drugs, stumbled down the street flipping off cars and yelling at passersby. When he moved along after fifteen minutes, One-Shot was thankful. His slitted eyes finally shut all the way, but every time he was on the verge of sweet oblivion, a car door would slam or someone would yell. Once, a woman pushing a shopping cart rolled by, the sound of the metal cart slicing into his brain for fifteen minutes.

The city spun around him, cars and buses and semi-trucks, yelling people, suffering people on the verge of death. With all the foot traffic around, he grew nervous, grabbed Grandpa's urn and hugged it to his chest. A pulse emanated from the urn, as if Grandpa's heart still beat within. He locked onto the heartbeat, counted the deep thumps, turned them into a song for his soul. In this way, he rode Grandpa's beating heart into the depths of slumber.

## Chapter 3: The Last Leg

When he awoke, he found himself refreshed, exhausted but refreshed. He glanced at the clock on his phone and saw he'd slept for two hours. It was still daylight but nearing the edge of it. He wanted to be out of the city before the sun went down. Rinsing his mouth out with a mouthful of soda, he studied Raven's instructions. He committed them to memory, closing his eyes and repeating the instructions line by line until he had memorized them.

He slid the key into the ignition, said a little prayer, and sighed when his car coughed to life. "Welcome back, old buddy. Not too much longer." He patted the dashboard, felt bad about abusing his friend. But that's the way it goes with friends sometimes, right?

With the memorized directions tumbling from his lips, he pulled out of the parking lot, waited for a shambling homeless dude to get out of the way, and then pulled back onto the road. After some trial and error, he followed the signs to I-5 and began his journey southward, breathing a sigh of relief as he left the twisted, depressing warren of roads that led through the city of Portland.

I-5 was a stress-free drive, boring but easy. The road ran straight as an arrow, hundreds of cars fish-schooling to hundreds of different locations. Semi-trucks, tall and plentiful, clogged the right lane of the three-lane highway. One-Shot rode in the middle, traveling a nice, breezy sixty-five miles per hour, cars speeding past him, giving him dirty looks for going the speed limit. One-Shot had come too far to start taking chances now.

His window-side arm was tan as hell after two days of near-constant sunshine. He didn't know how things worked in Oregon. It was…very white, which he inherently knew meant bad news for him. Better to go the speed limit and avoid the cops than get pulled over and have to explain himself. Plus, he didn't smell so good, had the busted window, and an urn full of Grandpa's ashes. He doubted the Oregon cops wouldn't want to see inside, and then he'd have to get mouthy, defend Grandpa's honor, and everyone knows what happens when a Native gets mouthy with the police. Nothing good.

The sun shone, and he tried to remember what day it was, resisting the urge to pull out his phone and check the date. It was low on battery, and he'd forgotten his charger at home like a dumbass. Maybe he could buy a cheap charger at a gas station along the way.

As he drove further away from Portland, the traffic dwindled, long lines of cars peeling off at various stops. First, Woodburn, then Salem, then Albany. Then it was his turn to exit. Once off I-5, the road turned into a two-lane highway, curvy, and overarched with foliage.

Shadows played on his windshield, and he squinted his eyes as he moved from shadow to light and back again. When he finished a cigarette, he tossed them in a half-empty Dr Pepper can in the cup holder. The tall grasses on the side of the road stood waist-high, ready to burn at a moment's notice. Sometimes he wanted to burn the world, but not today.

Occasionally, he'd drive through a small town, the houses large and run-down, old cars parked to rot in front yards. There was little to see out here, but it was better than the middle of the country where there was nothing but corn stretching out to the horizon. At least the twists and the turns of the road always offered the promise of something around the corner.

*I'm so tired,* Grandpa moaned.

"I know. I am too."

*I need to sleep.*

"You've been sleeping."

*I think I'm going to go soon.*

"Go where?"

*Don't know. Just know there's somewhere else to go.*

"Are you scared?"

*I'm hopeful.*

"Do you think you'll see people there? Grandma? Uncle Harry?"

*I hope so. Hope to see you there too one day, but long from now.*

One-Shot fell silent as did Grandpa who sounded weaker and weaker every time he spoke. He had to get him to the graveyard, and soon.

Eventually, even the houses gave way, the last stand of humanity bowing down before the awesomeness of Oregon's nature. Steep-sloped hills lined with trees as big around as his car rose to the sky, blotting out the sun. The highway pulsed onward, the road growing rougher out in the middle of nowhere. Now, in addition to the twisting and turning, it rose and fell, making his stomach lurch.

One-Shot felt as if he had left the world behind, stepped into a new dimension, a place of warm silence where the only sound was the sigh of wind through pine boughs and roots pushing through the rich, brown soil. In his mind, the road was a gateway; the only question—a gateway to what? Was Siletz a place full of magic, full of wandering spirits and mysticism, or was it a hell, a smaller scale version of the gross civility he had witnessed in Portland? Was it as depressing and weird as all those reservations he'd seen in movies and books, or was it somewhere in the middle?

He found "the middle" to be his least favorite option. He liked extremes. Go all in or don't even bother, like when he'd decided he was going to have a kid one way or another. He didn't choose the middle ground like everyone else would have done. He didn't go out and try and find another girl to fall in love with. No, he took love out of the equation. If he couldn't have one kid to love and raise, he would spawn a thousand children, even if he didn't have anything to do with them. Extreme was his preference, with the good and the bad.

Unfortunately, he was to be disappointed. Without any fanfare, the town of Siletz popped up out of nowhere. If the word "Siletz" hadn't been plastered on the sides of a few of the buildings, he wouldn't have known it was there. It took him less than three minutes to drive through the heart of town, and then, after crossing over a bridge spanning a shockingly blue river, he was forced to turn around when the road dumped him back into nature.

Spinning the wheel of the car around as he executed a three-point turn on the narrow highway, he prayed he wasn't about to get plastered by some Indian speeding down the road. But no one came, and he was able to turn around safely.

Taking it slower through town, One-Shot cruised, stopping at the town's lone gas station. Out front, two pumps stood uncovered and surrounded by an apron of gravel. A mini-mart off to the left of the pumps looked to be a good place to stop and get some information.

A tan man leaned against the side of the mini-mart, in no hurry to go anywhere. One-Shot nodded at him. He might be family after all.

Inside the mini-mart, he eyed a hot case stacked with cheap food—corn dogs, hot pockets, clearly not approved for individual resale, and burritos that looked harder than cement, the edges glowing orange from the grease seeping through the tortillas. They all called to One-Shot. Behind the counter, a large man sat, doughy, brown. Everywhere One-Shot looked, there were signs for Pepsi. He didn't know why. Didn't care. Maybe that's what soft drink companies did these days, cruised through small towns and gave them a pittance so they would only sell Pepsi products. It seemed to One-Shot there would be better things to do with money than put your signs up in a nowhere town like Siletz.

"Can I help you?" the man asked him.

One-Shot broke free from his thoughts. Clearly two hours of sleep hadn't brought him all the way back to the land of the living. "Yeah, I'm looking for a place to stay."

"Huh?"

"A hotel or something?"

The man nodded. "Well, there's no place around here like that. You want a hotel, you're gonna have to go back down that road about thirty minutes until you reach the ocean. Turn right. When you get to Newport, there's plenty of places to stay around there."

"No place here though?"

"If you got a tent, you can camp over by the river. But this time of year, with the powwow getting ready to start, all the spots are taken, I'm guessing."

One-Shot ran a hand through his hair.

"What's in the jar?" the man asked.

"Oh. My grandpa."

"You bringing him to the powwow?"

One-Shot had a vague idea of what a powwow was. "Yeah, something like that." One-Shot eyed the hot case, his mouth salivating at the prospect of actual food, even such as this. Then he remembered the Doozy he'd eaten in Wyoming. *Fuck it. Let's get extreme.* "Can I get a corn dog?"

The man behind the counter nodded, moved with the agonizing slowness of small-town folk, and shoved a corn dog in a paper sleeve. "That'll be one-fifty."

One-Shot pulled out his debit card, and the man looked at him like he was an idiot. "Cash only, my friend."

He reached into his wallet, leafed through the meager supply of cash he carried with him. He handed over the bills and waited as the man with the molasses for blood took his sweet-ass time making change.

"Thank you," he said.

"Yuh," the man mumbled.

One-Shot turned and left, the piping hot corn dog burning the pads of his fingers even through the paper sleeve. Though he wanted nothing more than to sleep, he knew he had to get the lay of the land.

Waiting for the corn dog to cool, he leaned against his car. One-Shot crossed his arms, the cornmeal-battered meat dangling from his hand by the wooden stick. He tried not to notice the man leaning against the wall, tried not to make eye contact with him and accidentally acknowledge his existence. However, it was a small town, and in small towns, even the lowest of the low knew when someone didn't belong.

"Come for the powwow?" the man asked.

The question was so clearly directed at One-Shot that he had no hope of pretending like he didn't hear the man. "Yeah."

"You got any money?"

The audacity of the man struck One-Shot as funny, and he figured maybe he wasn't all there in the head. "I got some, but it isn't free."

"Never is," the man said. Then he laughed, his smile revealing a few missing teeth.

"Tell you what," One-Shot said. "You give me some information, and I'll see if it was worth it."

"Sounds like a deal," the man said his hands together.

"First, can you tell me where the cemetery is?"

"Oh, that's easy. Take a right on Logsden Road, up that way, take a left on Government Hill, and then take a right on Cemetery. You'll see it."

One-Shot nodded. "Second, I'm out here on my own, been driving a long time. If you were out on the street and needed to park your car somewhere without getting bugged by cops, where would you park it?"

The man laughed, exposing his broken teeth once more. "Don't got no cops 'round here, but if I was in that situation, might take myself over to the skate park. Might be a little noisy now, but come nighttime, all those punks get up outta there, and no one thinks two seconds 'bout a car sitting there."

"Where's the skate park?"

"That's an easy one, too. Take a left on this street right here." He hiked a thumb at a green sign that read Swan Avenue. "Head on down, and you'll see it on your right."

With his non-corndog hand, One-Shot fished out his wallet. A deal was a deal. He produced a five-dollar bill and held it out to the man.

The man's hand open and closed, flapping to indicate he wanted more. One-Shot shrugged and fished out another five. The man went to snatch the bills from his hand, but at the last second, One-Shot pulled them out of his reach.

"One more question."

"Come on, come on," the man said, glowering like a disappointed five-year-old.

"At night, the cemetery, is it easy to get to?"

"What's that?"

"Like, are there fences, guards—that sort of thing?"

The man's eyes squinted as if One-Shot was up to something, which he was. Then the man's eyes flicked to the bills in his hands, and any sort of moral directive to protect the cemetery went out of his head. "No one up there at night. Hell, no one up there during the day most times. It's a sad place, quiet."

"Thank you," One-Shot said as he held the bills out to him.

The man snatched at them in case One-Shot pulled them away again. Without a word of thanks, he turned and headed inside the mini-mart. One-Shot smiled and laughed at the back of the departing man. He was strange but harmless.

By now, his corn dog had cooled to the point of being edible. He took a bite, crunching through the overcooked outside and immediately burning the roof of his mouth on the scorching mystery meat within.

When he finished, he followed the man's directions to the skatery. One-Shot's car groaned as it came to stop in a small lot that was half-grass and half-gravel. The concrete collection of dips and rails took up about as much space as a 7-11 parking lot. The kids in the park paid him no mind, and he tilted back his seat and fell asleep to the *click clack* of failed skateboard tricks.

# Chapter 4: Getting There

*Wake up, Palmer. They come for you.*

One-Shot sat up with a jolt, his arms flailing until his waking mind remembered where he was. *Someone was watching me.* It wasn't the dream, or Grandpa's warning that had woken him. It was the sensation of being watched. Sure enough, when he turned his head, he found the youths standing in the shadows, their faces hidden in gloom, the streetlight of the skate park pouring bright white light into One-Shot's eyes.

"You a faggot?" one of the kids asked. In the middle of their thighs, he spotted their shadowy hands holding their skateboards.

"Yeah, you fall asleep jacking off in there? You put it in that spittoon?" another kid asked, his voice dripping with anticipatory violence.

"What the hell are you talking about?" a third kid asked the second kid.

"You know, so he can save his jizz and put it on his toast or something."

"What the fuck?" the first kid asked. "Where do you come up with this shit?"

One-Shot sat up, grunting as he raised the seat of his car and contracted his abs. His left hand snaked into the side pocket of the driver's side door, felt cold metal. Without being obvious, he pulled the pistol up, got his fingers around the grip. Trying not to alert his inquisitors, he pulled it from the door pocket, kept it low so they couldn't see it. He'd only use it if he needed to, if the shadow of those skateboards came up high and blocked out the light.

"So, you a faggot or not?" the first kid asked when the third kid's shadow shrugged.

"You guys still use the word faggot out here?" One-Shot laughed, fishing a cigarette out of the console and flicking the wheel of his lighter a few times to get a better look at what he was dealing with here. Kids, pimply, brown skin—plain trash.

"Yeah, you shouldn't use that word," the second kid said.

"What word should he use, dipshit?" the third kid asked.

"Homosexual?"

"Ugh," the first kid said, "that sounds even worse." The first kid turned to him, his voice increasing in intensity. "You watching us and beating off, huh?"

One-Shot was already tired of the youths. "Nope. Drove cross-country and just needed a place to sleep."

The kids fell silent, taking it all in. One-Shot took a puff off the cigarette and blew the hot smoke into the air in the kid's direction.

"Can I bum one of those?" the tallest kid asked.

One-Shot shrugged, reached into the pack, and pulled one out. If a kid asks for a cigarette, you could be sure they already smoked them on their own. No harm there. He held the lighter out to the kid, but he said, "I got my own." The kid held the cigarette with the awkward stiffness of a new smoker, his fingers taut like soldiers on parade.

"Come on. Let's get out of here." the third kid said, the one who thought gay people jacked off in parking lots, saved jizz in an urn, and put it on toast when they got home.

"Hold up," the smoker said. "Can you buy us beer?"

"That I can't do."

"Alright," the tall kid said. "Thanks for the smoke."

The kids walked off, their shoulders slumped, their skateboards bouncing off their thighs. "Worth a shot," one of the kids said.

*They're coming for you.*

He remembered the words now, didn't know if they were imagined or real. He checked the time on his phone. Nine-thirty. He noted the battery remaining—fifteen percent. He flicked away the sweat pooled between his jaw and his neck.

His stomach gurgled at him. His jerky was gone, his Dr. Pepper supplies were low, but his mouth, dry and funky, ached for a different type of nourishment. He needed a drink—needed it bad.

On the way in, he'd passed a roadhouse, the type of place where everyone in town who had the thirst wound up. Might not be the best place to go and drink, but the only other option was to buy from the convenience store and drink in his car. While the crazy dude he'd mined for information earlier had said there were no cops, he didn't want to get busted for a DUI in a completely different state. That seemed like a fucking headache. He didn't know about Oregon, but in Pittsburgh, if they caught you drunk driving, you were fucked.

He leaned forward, digging in his pocket for his keys, his thirst intensifying by the second. With shaking hands, he drove the key home, turned the ignition, but nothing happened. *No, no, no.*

Panicking, he turned the key again. Nothing, not even the choking sound of the engine trying to turn over. The car was completely dead. "Fuck."

One-Shot reached up to the lights on his vehicle, felt them, turned them off. *Shit.* He cursed the signs on the highway, the ones that said lights were required to be on in a "safety corridor," whatever the hell that was. He'd forgotten to turn them off when he parked as it had still been daytime.

In the convenience store, he hadn't noticed any car batteries. "You're a fucking idiot," he chided himself.

Reaching down, One-Shot popped the trunk of his vehicle. He threw everything he still wanted inside—the remains of his Dr. Pepper and the instructions he needed to get back home. Everything else was garbage, a nice deterrent for anyone looking to fuck with his ride. *Just go up to the graveyard and get it done.* But he didn't. Without a vehicle to escape in, he didn't want to risk it. Then there was the problem of his courage. "Sorry, Grandpa."

*It's okay. I feel better,* Grandpa said. *I feel at home.*

His voice was different now, less weak.

"You have a good nap, Grandpa?"

*I slept forever. I sleep forever.*

"Yeah, I guess so. What say you and me go and get some food?"

*Oh, you can Palmer. I'm not hungry.*

"Okay."

With his car as secured as it was going to be, he placed Grandpa on the roof of the Accord and lit a cigarette. It was still warm outside, but after the stultifying heat of his car, it felt nice. In the distance, a cloud of his smoke floated underneath the streetlight, clinging together in the thick air.

He tucked his pistol down the back of his jeans, the cold metal kissing his ass cheek. The last thing he wanted was one of those stupid kids to come along, find the gun in his car, and blow out their own brains. *No cops. Yeah, right.*

One-Shot was asking for trouble carrying the thing around, but there was no way around it. Kicking gravel, he walked up the street, breathing in the fresh air like one recently released from prison. He set Grandpa down on the ground and lit another cigarette. With the cigarette dangling from his lips, he picked Grandpa up and carried him along the dark streets. Ahead, the moon hung bright in the sky.

Silently cursing, he crossed his fingers that the roadhouse was open. He had forgotten how small towns worked, how everything in them seemed to close by nine. But tonight, he was in luck. Light from the roadhouse's neon beer signs spilled across the street, and thumping music drifted on the night air.

With Grandpa clutched tight, he stepped inside. The smell of old, spilt beer assaulted his nose. A strand of flypaper hung behind the bar, its tacky surface peppered with slowly dying insects. Inside, the music wasn't as loud as he had expected. The walls of the roadhouse must be thin.

A red-haired man tended bar, filling up glasses and mixing drinks. Nothing fancy, just your basic rum and cokes and vodka and Red Bulls. Desby would put him to shame. The smell of deep fryers cloyed its way up One-Shot's nose, and his mouth began to water.

The red-haired man's eyes looked up at him once, clocked him for a stranger. In the midst of pouring something that smelled like detergent from a metal strainer, he cocked his head to a seat at the bar. One-Shot sat, and the bartender plopped a menu down. He was onto the next person before he could even crack the menu.

The bar's clientele was a mix of ages, races, and genders. To be honest, he'd expected more Natives on the property. What good was a reservation if white people could live there as well? It made no sense to him. Maybe the man with the red hair was Native, but he didn't look it.

He put the thought out of his mind. Decided he didn't want to judge lest he be judged. For all he knew, the dude behind the counter was King Indian—caught salmon, could hunt with a bow, all that shit. One-Shot couldn't do any of that. But he could get three sheets. That was one stereotype working in his favor.

The red-haired man returned. "What can I get ya?"

"Cheeseburger, fries, and a Bud."

The red-haired man set the beer on the counter and walked away.

Incomprehensible conversation buzzed under the bar's music. Periodically, loud laughter shattered the bar's calm. He recognized those laughs, knew them as a family trait. No one laughed as loud as his family. When they really got going in public, they were an embarrassment. Cackles—that's what those laughs were. He had one as well, but he hadn't used it in some time, hadn't found much funny over the last few years. As another peal of laughter rocked the bar, he wondered if it was a tribal trait. Even as he thought it, he turned to study the other people in the bar, sliding to a seat at the end of the bar, so he could study the people's faces without having to turn.

Behind him, one-half of the restaurant sat mostly empty, the dim lights falling on empty booths and tables. He supposed the roadhouse did more family-oriented business throughout the day, but at night, that half of the roadhouse sat abandoned. He tried not to be too conspicuous in his studies, but it turned out that was harder to do when you were carrying around an urn.

"Who's in the can?" one lady asked, sliding down the bar, moving from spinning stool to spinning stool, one at a time.

"My grandfather," he said, turning formal for some reason. Maybe it was because she was older, streaks of gray shooting through her hair.

"Anyone I know?"

One-Shot shrugged his shoulders, sipped his beer.

"Well, what was his name?" the woman asked.

She was probably a dozen years younger than Grandpa, and he doubted she'd know him, so he told her. "Oscar Lawrence." To most people, Grandpa's name wouldn't scream Native American, and he wasn't sure why it was, but none of the people from the tribe seemed to have "Native American" sounding names. It was too bad. One-Shot would have loved to have a name like Whitecloud or KickingAss.

The woman next to him, her hand clutching a tumbler wet with condensation, nodded her head as if she knew him. "I'm sorry to hear that. May he find his way in the afterlife."

"Yeah," One-Shot said, not feeling particularly spiritual at the moment.

"You gonna bury him up at the cemetery?" the woman asked.

For some reason, she seemed to hang on his every word, as if she was far too interested in what was going on with him and Grandpa. But then again, he had just driven across country thinking country music was coming out of the fillings in his molars, so he could be reading her wrong altogether. He didn't know what he could trust anymore. Didn't know if he was losing it or had just driven himself to exhaustion. He needed to get back home, get among familiar faces, settings, and routines to find out if he'd permanently cracked.

"I'm sorry if I'm intruding," the woman said.

It was then that One-Shot realized he hadn't bothered answering the woman. "It's fine," he said by way of apology. "I was just thinking. But yeah, the cemetery for Grandpa."

She nodded her head. "Well, I'll leave you to it then. See you at the powwow tomorrow, I suppose." With that, she went stool hopping away from him before he could even tell her he wasn't planning on attending.

Left to his own devices, One-Shot concentrated on drinking his beer and testing his own sanity. By the time the bartender returned with his food, he hadn't decided if he was nuts or not. He supposed it wasn't up to him. Sanity wasn't an issue for the crazy. It was only a problem for those around them. Society would decide if he was nuts or not.

One thing he did know, the roadhouse chef knew how to make a mean fucking burger. It wasn't big, but it had a nice peppery flavor, the edges of the patty smashed flat, cooked until it developed a satisfying crispiness. A slice of good, old-fashioned American cheese dripped down the sides. He'd been to restaurants where they threw an expensive slice of cheddar or five-year-aged gouda on a burger… Those were always a letdown. Normal cheese turned oily and lost its flavor upon melting. But not American cheese. American cheese got better as it melted.

The fries sucked though. They had probably come from a bag and been shoved into a deep fryer. Crinkle cuts…psshh. There were better cuts for a potato out there.

When One-Shot finished his burger, leaving most of the fries untouched, he ordered another beer. When the glass sat empty but for a slime of foam on the side he paid up and left.

As he walked from the roadhouse, his belly full, and Grandpa snoring fitfully under his arm, he failed to notice the eyes following him out the door. He didn't notice the hubbub of the restaurant dying off completely or the people tracking his exit. If he would have turned around as he walked back to his car, he would have found them at the windows, their eyes glued to his back, locked in silence.

Back at his car, he smoked once more, while Grandpa sat on the hood.

*How did it taste?* Grandpa asked.

"Delicious."

*Mmmm.*

"Are you hungry?"

*Just tired.*

"Not too much longer now," he said as he blew smoke into the air. The insects around him chirped and buzzed, and he felt like the only person on the planet, with the exception of Grandpa, but he wasn't really even a person anymore.

When he finished, he tossed the cigarette butt to the gravel and ground it out with his shoe. He would have picked it up and put it in his ash can in the car, but the ground was already littered with cigarette butts, probably dropped from the dirty fingers of rebellious youths.

"Well, shall we get this over with?"

*Sleepy time.*

With no shovel in his possession, not even a garden trowel, he tucked Grandpa under his arm once more and headed toward the cemetery. A left on the main drag, a right, and then another left, and he'd be there. He'd be out of Siletz by tomorrow morning. He'd have to get a jump start, but he should be alright after that.

The night clung tight to him, the shadows deep and blue-black. Tall grasses swished against his jeans as he walked across a field leading from the skate park to the road. *Better to keep off the road altogether.* A lone man walking in this sleepy town was noticeable enough, a man with an urn tucked under his arm even more so.

The grass pressed against his jeans, pushing back against him, urging him to turn around and go home. But he couldn't. Grandpa was getting thinner now, dwindling away to nothing. If he didn't get him in the ground, he might be lost forever.

A haunting whistle cut through the night, gliding across the still air, coming from everywhere and nowhere all at once. He turned left and right, scanning for the source of the whistle. There! On the other side of the field, leaning against his car, he spotted the brown man in the broad-brimmed hat whistling through his pursed lips.

The grass swished even louder against his legs as One-Shot broke into a trot, his armpits releasing a surge of adrenaline-soaked perspiration. He tripped on something hidden in the grass, something metal and clunky. More concerned by the consequence of his trip than with the source, he searched around him, peering through the tall grasses, trying to locate the Whistle Man.

The light of the skate park's streetlamp barely reached out here. He might be hidden if he didn't move. The whistle, like the warble of a bow driven across the edge of a singing saw, made the hair on his neck stand up. One-Shot pushed himself to his feet, checking the duct tape of Grandpa's urn subconsciously. When he stood, he found the Whistle Man patiently standing five feet away.

He looked different now, the broad-brimmed hat gone, replaced by the man's gray-black hair, parted in the middle and hanging down his shoulders in two thin braids. A bone-beaded chest piece hung over a black shirt decorated with silver spirals. The man said nothing, and for a moment, the two men stood locked in a staring contest. The shadow of the Whistle Man's brow hid his eyes, and One-Shot peered into those black pools, trying to find something human.

*Don't go,* Grandpa warned. *It's not worth it.*

Even the bugs paused to see who would win the staring contest. Who would blink? Who would lose face? The crickets wanted to know, and they stopped rubbing their legs together, waiting with bated breath.

Finally, One-Shot couldn't stand it. He was sweating buckets, exhausted, and tired of dealing with the Whistle Man. "Fuck it," he said, breaking eye contact. He took a step to his left, and the Whistle Man stepped with him. One-Shot hesitated, tried to see the man's eyes once more, but the shadows were too deep. He reached out to shove the man, to find out if he was real, and he tumbled right through his body as if he was made of cigarette smoke.

One-Shot's head rocked back, and the muscles in his body tensed up as if he had grabbed hold of a live wire. Then he was falling into the thick grass.

He shook his head as the images in his mind piled up like the pebbles and stones at the bottom of a rocky slope. One-Shot saw the man across the sea, amid unfamiliar plants and strange people, sneaking through the humid jungle, crouched among the underbrush, scouring the ground for land mines and tripwires. He moved with his back hunched and aching. But to straighten his back was to give in, to lose focus. That's when people died, when people blew up, when their bodies turned into red clouds, and their legs and flesh stained the jungle for a twenty-yard radius. Better to ache than to become a human cloud.

One-Shot put out a hand and straightened his body, pushing himself off the ground, his free arm questing for the coldness of Grandpa's urn. His hands brushed against the cold brass as the pop of ancient gunfire reached his ears.

The gunshots echoed across time and space, but only One-Shot heard them. In his mind, he saw the source of those gunshots, spotted the muzzle flashes through the trees, knew the time for caution was long gone. He ran, his arms pumping, not worried about turning into a blood cloud anymore. Better the quick end of a landmine than the slow torture of the enemy.

He ran, his weapon forgotten. His boots wet, his feet aching with fungal rot, he plowed through the jungle, fully committing to his fear. Onward he fled, wide-fronded jungle plants blocking off the view of the world around him and smacking him across his face for his cowardice.

One-Shot coughed in the night, hacking up the metallic-tinged phlegm of someone gorging on fear. He leaned forward, thick drool and lung butter clinging to his chin. His brain felt like it was ripping apart as it tried to exist in two realities at once.

Then he burst into a clearing, a place where enemy soldiers puttered about, loading weapons, eating food from a steaming pot while they had the opportunity. Their heads turned in his direction, their skin tone eerily similar to his own. They yelled at him in a language he couldn't comprehend, and he yelled back. They plucked their rifles from the ground, aimed, and fired. The bullets entered his body—a dozen punches. He only had a few moments to feel the pain, and then something smacked into his forehead. The world went dark.

In the darkness, time flowed around him as if he were a jutting boulder in the middle of a river. Over years, the fungi, the bacteria, and the worms sawed away his flesh, ate it, digested it, and shit it out all around him. Bit by bit, he felt himself taken away, dripping through the ground over the course of decades, washed away by the rain, evaporated into the sky until he became so thin he lost all the things he once remembered, but for the call of home. He lost the language his fellow soldiers spoke. He lost the memory of the way home, but then, he felt something calling him. One-Shot...and his blood.

*What about the blood?*

One-Shot struggled free of the darkness, tried to make sense of the world around him. Grass, not jungle, streetlights, not hot sun and humidity. He fumbled for the urn and spun to face the Whistle Man, who stood with his lips pursed together, the shadows of his eyes boring into One-Shot's soul.

One-Shot turned and ran from him, the story of the Whistle Man's life fading like a bad dream. Across the field he scrambled, clutching Grandpa.

The Whistle Man followed, though his body was thousands of miles away, moldering in a jungle, worms and other insects crawling over his fleshless bones.

"Come along then," One-Shot shouted in challenge. "Come along!"

He huffed across the field, trying to remember the last time he had run. The muscles in his legs, long neglected, good only for standing behind a bar or in front of it, stretched painfully. At the edge of the field, he hopped from the grass to the unevenly paved road. It had the feel of a road paved by amateurs—dips, rises, and potholes acted as land mines. He ran onward, listing from side to side like a drunken sailor, knowing if he fell, he wouldn't rise again.

Sprinting across the main road like a bounding elk, he didn't even pause to see if the way was clear. The generic houses gave way to trees that grew thick and tall.

Still, the whistle pierced his ears and drove into his brain, a song he could almost understand. The world tilted upward now, a hill rising in front of him. The curbs on the sides of the road were painted red, and great evergreens, their trunks as thick as bridge pylons, rocketed up into the sky.

# Chapter 5: The Cemetery

He was on the reservation proper now, but not the way he'd wanted to be. He'd wanted to appear solemn and dutiful, proud. Instead, he ran panting and terrified.

Each step burned, and Grandpa's urn seemed to weigh more and more the closer he came to his goal. Ahead the cemetery gate loomed, a simple light hanging from a wooden pole illuminating a sign. He didn't read it, didn't care. All he wanted to do was get there and end this nightmare.

He tripped over the curb, and Grandpa's urn tumbled from his hands, rolling across the ground and into the shadows.

*Help!* Grandpa called.

One-Shot glanced over his shoulder, caught sight of the Whistle Man plodding in his direction, his arms held out to the side, palms up, as if ready to receive a gift. "Well, come on then!" One-Shot screamed.

He pushed himself up and rushed over to the area where Grandpa's urn had disappeared. Bending down, he fumbled his hands through ferns growing placidly at the base of a tree. His hand touched something metallic, and he dove forward, trusting it was the urn. He picked it up and ran, unable to see the names of the graves in the dark.

"Which one is it, Grandpa? Huh? Which one?"

*I don't know.*

One-Shot's frustration mounted. He thought to leave then, to abandon his mission completely. Perhaps he could come back during the day, when people were around. The tribe wouldn't like him digging in the earth, burying Grandpa without rites and ceremonies, and whatever the hell else his tribe did, but fuck 'em.

Ready to flee, One-Shot turned and watched as the Whistle Man stepped onto the cemetery's grass. He walked as one accepting a gift. When his foot touched the edge of the cemetery, his body glowed a bright blue.

The Whistle Man's tune rose and fell, and he stalked across the graves with no care for physical impediments. He plowed through a tombstone like it was made of dreams, his body pushing through the granite. Onward he stalked, veering away from One-Shot, who only now understood the man had never been after him. His body, traveling for years, had needed a guide, and he'd latched onto One-Shot somehow, or maybe onto Grandpa.

As if someone had flipped a switch, his fear vanished. He rose, the urn under his arm. One-Shot followed the man across graves decorated with flowers, little American flags, and the occasional eagle feather. Dreamcatchers hung from the corners of a few grave markers. He avoided looking at the names of the dead, didn't want any other spirits following him around.

The Whistle Man's tune changed, grew less sorrowful and more hopeful. One-Shot followed him to a forlorn grave, neglected and forgotten. This grave had no decorations on it. The gray granite sat heavy and plain, but for a brass nameplate decorated with an American flag. The Whistle Man fell to his knees, placed his hands to the dirt, and then followed with his head. He crawled forward, pushing his way into the earth. His boots, worn from decades of wandering, disappeared, and the blue-white light vanished with him, plunging One-Shot into darkness. By the last of the light, he had caught a name and a date, but they meant nothing to him.

*He's home,* Grandpa said.

One-Shot patted his pockets but couldn't find his medicine. He'd left the cigarettes back at his car. "I'm fucking losing it." The sad part was he could never tell anyone about his encounter. Who would believe him? There was no proof but for the scars on his soul, and only a few people in this world could see those. Maybe Sadie could. He could tell Sadie anything.

*I'm tired,* Grandpa said.

"I know," One-Shot comforted. "Let's put you to bed."

One-Shot dug in his pocket and pulled out his cell phone. He glanced around the dimly lit cemetery. He scanned the graveyard, wondering if the feeling of being watched was all in his mind. Were the dead listening, watching his every move?

He turned on his phone's flashlight to check the borders of the cemetery to see if anyone was going to come and stop him. But no one was there, though the back of his neck crawled as if eyes were locked upon him.

Methodically, he strode up and down the rows of graves, searching for the right name. He tried not to see the dates on the graves, tried not to notice all the ones who had died younger than him. One-Shot had never expected to live as long as he had. Thirty had seemed like an impossibility as a youth, so far away. But here he was, doing the things thirty-year olds had to do, getting used to death and putting away loved ones, clinging to their memories so they didn't disappear forever.

*Who will remember me?*

*No one. They'll all be gone by the time I die. I have no one, just Raven.* She would remember him, but when she was gone, One-Shot would go with her, disappearing forever. Nothing he'd done would last… Except for those kids, kids he didn't know, kids who would never know him. Would they grow up always wondering about him?

*We all make mistakes,* Grandpa said.

One-Shot's flashlight slid across the graves, his eyes squinting to make out the shadowy letters. "Did you make mistakes, Grandpa?"

*Many and more. Many and more.*

"Tell me."

*It's a long story, and my time is short. I can feel myself being pulled to the next place.*

"Tell me a little."

*You may not like what you hear.*

"If you say it, I'll always like it."

Grandpa fell silent, and it was then that One-Shot discovered the grave. "May Lawrence." Her grave was nothing special, nothing different than the other graves he'd seen. Off to the side sat the grave of his Uncle Harry. Harold Lawrence had lived from 1962-1983. He died the same year as his grandmother. "But that's not right."

*Oh, it is, my Palmer, my Palmer, my beautiful Palmer.*

"I don't understand." For his entire life, he'd been told they had died at different times, that his uncle had been hit by a car, that he'd been walking drunk down the road and stepped in front of a moving car. They called it suicide. As far as Grandma went, he'd just assumed she'd passed away peacefully. But seeing the years, he understood she had been too young for that.

*They wanted him, needed him to make things right, to restore the balance.*

"What does that mean?"

*I'm tired, Palmer.*

One-Shot nodded his head, bent down on the flat soil of Grandma's grave, and began digging with his bare hands. The grass was scrubby, the earth filled with pine needles. The soil came away in great clumps that stabbed his palms. As he dug, tears came to his eyes, and he hoped no one would come along and see him like this, wearing his sorrow so plain on his face. When he had dug a deep enough hole, his hands sore and bleeding, he ripped the duct tape off the urn. He reached inside, tore open the plastic bag containing Grandpa and then upended him into the shallow grave.

"I hope you can sleep now."

*Goodbye, Palmer. I love you. Tell everyone else I love them too.*

Overcome with emotion, all One-Shot could do was nod his head.

As he filled in the grave, he sang Grandpa one last song, The Stanley Brothers' words dripping from his mouth, heavy with sorrow, mourning, and a longing to defy nature's seeming distaste for never-ending life. When he finished, he patted the grave flat, lay on it, putting his ear to the ground to see if he could hear Grandma and Grandpa talking.

That's when they found him.

# Chapter 6: Powwow

They fell upon him rough and bruising. When they jerked him to his feet by his hair, he discovered they were people like him—brown-skinned, their mouths bowing downward to show their disapproval of his actions. Twenty people, maybe more. It struck him funny that there should be so many.

A stout woman stood before him. Though she was shorter than him, she felt taller. Her gray hair glowed in the night, and light reflected off her eyeglasses. She walked among the others with an air of superiority. The others in the group, of all ages, shapes, and sizes, looked toward her, waiting for her to speak.

The woman smiled, her eyes shrinking into slits through which black eyeballs glittered. The smile scared him, and he tried to shake free of those holding him in place, tried to run for his car a mile away.

*The gun.*

He could do it. Break an arm free and pull his handgun out and start blasting, but then... Then what? Then he'd be a murderer. A grave defiler was bad enough, but if he did time, it wouldn't be for long, not once the circumstances were known. If he killed people, he'd go away for life.

"You came back," the woman said. But she wasn't speaking to One-Shot, she spoke to the grave. She spat on the ground. "A curse on you."

One-Shot's anger flared quick and hot, and he tried to shake free of his captors, but the men who held him were strong and young. Their fingers dug into his flesh, and they shook him into compliance, one of them cuffing him on the back of his head.

The woman turned to him. "Arnold Yeager. So nice to meet you."

He had nothing to say. She nodded as if this were a wise move. Then they placed a bag over his head and led him from the cemetery.

He stumbled down a curb, across pavement, up another curb, and then through flat grass. Through the bag, he sensed a flickering fire in the distance. He kept his mouth closed, positive something worse than a jail cell awaited him.

They sat him down on a metal bench of some sort. All around, boots clanked off metal risers as his captors took seats around him.

The bag clung to his sweaty face, and he thought he was going to scream if they didn't remove it soon. With every breath he took, the bag tried to climb its way up his nostrils. It wasn't quite burlap, but not far off.

Someone whispered into his ear, and he jumped—the voice of the woman, the elder with the glittering black eyes.

"It's good you came back."

Her breath burned his ear.

"Things haven't been the same since your grandfather left."

"What are you talking about?" he gasped. His fear crawled all over him, like ants, small and insignificant until you realized they were on every inch of your skin. One-Shot yearned to stand up and slap at his arms. If he could only see, everything would be alright. He reached up to remove the bag, and someone behind him kicked him in the head with the hard sole of a boot. He let his hand drop, allowed his hell to continue.

"Your grandfather is known to us. Your whole family is known to us. You see, he carries the Old Blood, the gift of the gods."

"You're crazy," One-Shot said.

The woman laughed, a husky thing. "No, you are. That's the curse of the Old Blood. Special, but harmful. Good and bad. Balance, you see?"

*The gun. I can blast my way out of here. This is some Wicker Man shit I stumbled right into, and now it's going to be the bees for me, and I'm not even allergic.* What was that? That buzzing? *The bees.*

"Since your grandfather abandoned us so long ago, we've struggled as a people. The Old Blood is a gift and a curse. Oscar Lawrence took it from us, left us with only the curse."

One-Shot didn't give two fucks about gifts, or about Old Blood and gods. He'd never seen a god; his blood had never done shit for him but keep his heart pumping and his cock throbbing. "What are you going to do to me?"

"What should have been done long ago. We're going to give you the choice. But first, we have to purify you."

They ripped the bag from his head. The buzzing drew closer. *The bees.* He screamed while the people around him laughed. He felt something cold against his scalp, dragging across his skin, and then a cloud of something drifted across his eyes—his own hair. He tried to look at the woman to his left, the woman with the lava breath, but rough hands gripped him, kept his head straight. His hair came off in clumps as the clippers scraped across his scalp.

From somewhere, the sound of drums began, rhythmic—ocean deep. His heart synced up to the beat, helping him control his fear. *I still have the gun. If I need to, I can do it.*

Chanting began, joining the sounds of the drums, high-pitched and wailing. He realized he knew the song, had heard the Whistle Man whistling the tune across the country. The song rose and fell, deep pits and valleys followed by plaintive war-like cries. There were no words—not that he recognized—but he could make out the emotions.

In front of him, a group of people appeared, dressed in fancy, jingling clothing, the firelight reflecting off the metal bells stitched to their garments.

"What is this?"

"The powwow," Lava Breath said.

"I thought it didn't start until tomorrow."

"That ones for the white people. This is the one for us, the real powwow. If you're lucky, you'll hear the voice of the gods, feel it speaking through your blood."

One-Shot fell silent, his eyes glued to the flames. People, their faces painted, their clothing bouncing hypnotically, whirled around the fire. They stomped to the beat of the drum, spinning, lifting their heads up to the sky and then returning their focus to their feet—balance, everywhere balance.

A woman came and sat before him with a bowl of dye in her hands. She reached in with her bare fingers and spread the mixture on his cheeks. It smelled pungent, strong, and his head began to swim.

Lava Breath whispered secrets to him, about how his grandfather had broken the tribe, how when his son Harold had exhibited the touch of the gods, he'd been approached, told he was the one to lead the tribe spiritually. But as always, there was a price to pay for the benefit of the tribe.

"He didn't want to pay this price."

"What was the price?"

"He had to strengthen the link between the blood and the gods."

One-Shot tried to puzzle out the mystery of her words, tried to figure out what "strengthen the link" meant, but his thoughts were dark. "How do you strengthen the link?"

"You have to sever the other links."

The woman finished smearing the paste on his face and smiled at him. He didn't smile back.

The drums beat faster, and his heart, caught up in the moving rhythm, tried to escape his chest.

"You've been busy, One-Shot," Lava Breath said.

On the far end of the field, in the shadows, they appeared, one by one, carrying bundles in their arms, small, wriggling bundles.

"No," he whispered.

"It must be done. For the tribe."

"No," he said louder this time.

The people came closer. They were dressed in jeans and shirts with band names printed on them, regular clothes for regular people. Somehow this made it worse.

"You've felt it," Lava Breath said, "the call of the tribe. Why else would you make so many?"

One-Shot shook in his seat, his fists clenched.

"Strengthen the bonds," Lava Breath implored, her voice cooing, as if she were talking to a baby.

"I won't."

Lava Breath gripped his arm as a woman with long black hair and a smooth face knelt before him, holding out a baby as an offering.

"This isn't mine," he said.

In One-Shot's hand, Lava Breath placed a blade, stone and rough, its edge chipped to a keenness no manufactured blade could match.

"They are all yours."

He didn't want to count them, but he couldn't resist. Fifteen bundles, squirming and wriggling, some larger than others. The largest was no bundle at all, but a chubby-cheeked little boy, walking on his own, his eyes wide, the confusion of toddlerism plastered to his face.

"Fuck." The word slipped from his lips.

"And so you did," Lava Breath said. The heat of her voice assaulted him, her breath working through his ear canal and into his brain, scrambling his thoughts.

"I'm going crazy," he said. "That's all this is. I'm losing my mind."

"You did it to yourself. Each one of these bastards weakened your link to the gods, took what you were and made you lesser. Restore the link, guide us. You will never want; you will be revered. Sacrifice for us."

The mere thought of hurting those children made One-Shot want to throw up. He dropped the knife from his hand,

and it fell to the ground. The woman at his knees smiled up at him still, and Lava Breath leaned in closer. He could feel the cracks in her dry lips against his ear.

"There is another way," she purred. "Will you choose it?"

"Anything. Anything." Tears sprang to his eyes, and she nodded.

"You must do the walk."

"I'll walk to the fucking moon. Just don't make me hurt those babies."

Her forehead pressed against his bare scalp, and One-Shot squeezed his eyes closed. The music stopped and the woman holding the baby vanished. *Had she ever been there to begin with?* The dancers stood regarding him, the sweat of their exposed skin glistening in the firelight, their chests heaving. All around, silence fell. Lava Breath placed a hand like fire on his arm and pulled him to his feet.

"He's going to do the walk!" she pronounced.

At this, the members of the tribe clasped their hands together and held them to the sky.

The drums began again, pounding deeper, faster. There was a meaning in those drums, something he couldn't quite grasp, but it drove him. Without being bidden, he walked forward, kicking the stone knife to the side with his shoe.

The people parted for him, forming a corridor of flesh to his left and right. He wended his way along the path made of people, looking at the face of each one. Somehow, with all this going on, they managed to smile at him, and for a moment, he thought, maybe he would be welcomed here. Maybe this was his home. When he made eye contact with the people, some of them gasping and sweating, they nodded back at him, a reverence in their eyes.

"Thank you," a man with long braids said.

One-Shot processed onward, not knowing what to say to the grateful man.

The people closed in around him as he passed, cutting off any escape. From the corner of his eye, he saw Lava Breath walking to his right. One of the women blew him a kiss, but he ignored it. There was nothing romantic about this whole situation for One-Shot. As soon as he was out of the gauntlet, he would run, head for the heart of town. Anyone who got in his way would wind up with a bullet in the belly.

The light of the fire dimmed the further he went. Ahead, the people faded away to be replaced by trees, thick and ancient, their bark red and rich. He was about to run when Lava Breath put a hand on his shoulder and pulled him to a stop.

"Don't leave the path," she said. His ear felt like it was going to melt from the embrace of her breath.

"Why?"

"Advice is given. Reasons are not."

One-Shot tired of her mystery. He bet if he found Lava Breath in the roadhouse on a Saturday evening, her sparse-word, wise-Indian act would be all gone. She'd be laughing it up and talking just like everyone else. A fucking act; that's all it was.

"Go now. Find your way out before the sun comes up."

"What happens if I'm not out in time?"

"We will never see you again." Lava Breath shoved him, pushed him toward the forest.

One-Shot stumbled backward. *He didn't want to go into the forest.* He had no idea what was waiting for him, but he didn't like the insinuation he might not be coming out alive.

"This is like some shit you reservation Indians play on city Indians, right? Oh, ha ha! You motherfuckers got me." One-Shot clapped slowly.

The brown people he'd passed watched him, their heads backlit by the huge bonfire. They smiled, not in a mocking way, but in a truly appreciative way.

"I'm gonna go in there, and one of you motherfuckers is gonna jump out and try and scare me, right? Well, I'm warning you. Anyone who does is gonna get their ass kicked. You understand?"

Not a word. Just that appreciative look, as if he held within his heart all the answers to their prayers.

The thought crossed his mind to call their bluff, to run back through the gauntlet, wave his handgun around, but he feared that course of action. He was fairly sure this was all some sort of elaborate prank. It was either that, or he was going completely fucking nuts, his mind conjuring some weird, alternate universe.

A rock hit him in the chest, and he flinched. He stared into the crowd, hurt, trying to find the person who had assaulted him.

Another rock sailed in his direction, hitting him in the shoulder. Then more came, and he turned and ran. Behind him, the drums picked up again, and the singing began. It sounded oddly joyful.

# Chapter 7: Spirit Walk

*Those weren't my babies. No fucking way. How would they even get them? Have they been watching me? Keeping track of my comings and goings?* He thought about the ever-present homeless men in his city, the ones with the brown skin, always looking, always present. Were they spies for his tribe?

The path in front of him varied between two and three people wide. The ground was dark, packed earth, mixed with shredded bark, either put down on purpose or dropped by the trees naturally over the centuries. Nowhere did anything green grow.

The boughs of the trees interlocked, blocking out the sky. Between the tree trunks, gnarled bits of underbrush sprung up, forming a dense barrier of tangled branches. Together, the trees, the underbrush, and the floor combined to make an unbreachable tunnel. One-Shot hated everything about this place, except for the smell. Something about the dry, earthy air tickled something in the primordial regions of his brain. That smell tried to tell him not to be afraid. *You're just going home.* Despite the reassuring thought, One-Shot *was* scared, terrified this was all some dark joke with him as the punchline. He knew how punchlines worked in these situations… The joke was always death. Always.

As the path twisted, the people at the other end of the tunnel disappeared, along with the orange light of the fire. Once out of sight, One-Shot rushed to a space between two huge tree trunks, pressed himself into the jagged foliage between. He came away with scratches on his arms and face.

The only relief he received for his effort was knowing that if he couldn't get out, none of them could get in.

*The trees.*

As he walked, he scanned for a tree he could climb, a low-hanging branch within reach, a trunk twisted and gnarled enough to allow him to climb upward. Nothing presented itself, and after passing half-a-mile of unscalable tree trunks and impassable undergrowth, he grew desperate.

He picked a tree and ran toward it, knowing he risked a broken ankle in the dark. His shoes scraped against the tree bark, and up he went, climbing into the air, his arms reaching upward for one of the tree branches. Gravity took him, wrapped its weighty arms around his body, and threw him back to the ground. He landed with a thud and lay there.

*I can just sit here. More people should do that in movies. Just sit there, and it will all go away. But no, the idiots always run crying and screaming into the waiting jaws of death.*

He dusted his hands off, feeling small, imperceptible splinters in his palms from the barky floor.

A gray light approached further down the path. It looked like the foaming edge of an ocean wave, but it moved with the speed of an uncoordinated two-year-old on a tricycle, jerking and twisting its way toward him.

The wave rose, rearing back like a horse and billowing into the sky.

He could have run, could have escaped the leading edge of the fog, but he let it wash over him. *If I can't see them, then they can't see me.*

The kiss of the fog was colder than he expected, and immediately, his skin turned icy. His teeth chattered, and he stood, walking deeper along the tree-lined path lest he froze in place. As he walked, he rubbed his hands along his arms to create warming friction, but still his teeth clacked.

From his right, there came a *thump*. He jumped, pulling his handgun from his waistband. Another *thump* followed, and then another. Something fell from the sky and hit him in the head. He screamed and hopped backward. Craning his head back, he raised his pistol in the air. By the light of the mist, he spotted shadows falling from the sky. One fell to his right, and he crouched down, his hand pawing along the ground until he found what had fallen from above. He picked it up and held it close to his face. The squirrel in his hand was cold, its body already stiff with death. Disgusted, he dropped it on the ground and rubbed his hand on his jeans as the forest rained corpses upon him. Something beaked and winged hit him in the shoulder, and he took off running, panicking once more.

In his mind, he imagined a bunch of brown men in loin cloths covering their mouths with their hands to suppress laughter as they dropped small, deceased animals down upon One-Shot. "Fuckers."

Onward he ran, fully expecting to smack headfirst into a tree trunk, but the time never came. Though the mist had chilled him, running warmed him up, and his body grew wet with slimy, anxious sweat, his shirt clinging to his chest. The gun in his hand seemed to weigh more with every step.

The ground sloped downward. The path twisted left then right, the fog thickening until he felt as if he was running through the innards of a pillow. His breath came in ragged gasps, and still the forest pelted him with birds, squirrels, and chipmunks.

If there was one thing One-Shot knew, it was that he was going to be filthy rich after he got through this ordeal. The tribe would have one hell of a lawsuit on its hands…although, he was on the reservation…and it was a sovereign nation and all, but every real Indian knew that sovereign nation thing was bullshit. Sure, if you played by the government's rules and kissed their ass, they'd let you be "sovereign" as hell. But as soon as something went down, as soon as they found resources on your land or someone acted out against the government, you could ball that sovereignty up and wipe your ass with it. Try being sovereign when some fucking company wants to pipe a trillion billion tons of oil through your land; keep playing that card until you can't stop laughing.

He was laughing about suing his tribe when he stepped into the coldest water puddle of his life. The liquid topped the sides of his boots, filling up all the space in his shoe. The mist swirled around him so he couldn't see the surface, and somehow, this made it worse. Shivering, he tried to back out of the frigid liquid, but when he backed away, he found himself sinking deeper. He turned to the side, thinking maybe he had lost his bearings. Taking a long step forward, he found himself submerged even more. Now the water came to his shin, the cold licking like razorblades against his skin.

He spun in a circle, tried to peer through the fog, even going so far as to try and bail the mist out of the way with his hands. All this did was set it swirling. Rather than risk another errant step, One-Shot bent down, waved his arms through the water to feel for the ground. "Jesus Christ," he muttered as the cold water enveloped his hands and forearms. Bent over at a ninety-degree angle, One-Shot tried dragged his palms across wet mud, trying to ascertain which way the ground sloped. As he splashed his hands, he discovered nothing, as if he stood on an isolated point of land submerged in the middle of a great sea.

Hopelessness constricted One-Shot's chest, and his eyes began to water. He glared up at the sky, hidden behind a veil of mist. The water flowed around his feet, and the point of land he stood upon melted away with every breath. Through the veil of white, the sound of crying reached his ears. The high-pitched keening intensified, and he put his hands to his ears, his lips drawn back in a pained grimace.

The plaintive crying intensified, elevating in pitch until it became so sharp his teeth ached. One-Shot was sure if it grew any higher, his teeth would shatter like a champagne glass at the voice of a master opera singer.

From above, on the other side of the blinding mist, a chant began as tribal drums approached. They uttered a single harsh syllable. Together, a hundred voices chanted. "Chum!"

*Chum! Chum! Chum!*

He didn't know if it was a tribal word or not, didn't know word one of his tribe's language. "Stop!" he called, his panic pressing him into action as the icy water's current eroded the muddy point on which he stood. Every second, he sunk lower. The water lapped against the knee of his jeans now.

*Chum! Chum! Chum!* Drums banged like thunder in the sky.

The water touched his thigh now. One-Shot pulled his phone from his pocket, flipped it open, and tried to dial the police. *There are no police in Siletz.* But he didn't even know if he was in Siletz anymore. How long had he been walking through the mist before he came to this godforsaken river? *Ocean? Lake?* No matter. His phone had no signal. He closed his eyes and bashed the phone against his forehead.

*Chum! Chum! Chum!*

The crying of babies grew into a painful roar, like standing next to a jet engine. Then, one by one, the crying stopped, voices fading away until all that remained was the chanting tribe.

*Chum! Chum! Chum!*

The water next to him exploded, dousing his face with water. The cold droplets burned his skin. Another splash and another explosion of water, then more, and more. The water's surface boiled as if someone had dropped a moon's worth of dry ice into it.

Then the smell hit him—unpleasant, familiar.

Something bumped into his waist where the water lapped against the belt of his jeans. Frightened, his mind conjuring all sorts of images, One-Shot slapped at the thing, pulling something cold and soft from the water. He grabbed it, thinking to wring the life out of whatever river monstrosity had come to take a bite out of him, for he was sure his tribe meant to feed him to the river. *I am the chum.*

But then he looked at what he held in his hand, twisted it and turned it by the light of the fog. When he realized what it was, a sick sob escaped his lips, and he tossed the chunk of flesh into the water.

"You bastards!" he called.

*Chum! Chum! Chum!* came the response. More bits of flesh splashed around him.

"You sick bastards!"

He would have continued shouting, but somewhere off in the fog, he heard the glide of something large knifing through the water. *They're coming for me.*

One-Shot pulled his pistol free, aimed it upward at the chanting, invisible people in the mist.

He pulled the trigger, punctuating each pull with a curse for the murderers above. The pistol thundered, the flash of his handgun lighting up the mist like lightning in the sky. Nothing happened, only more of that rippling water sound, more chanting, more bits of flesh bumping against his body.

One-Shot pressed the barrel of his handgun to his forehead and felt his flesh sizzle under the heat. With his eyes squeezed shut, his mouth began to mutter, capturing and holding onto sounds that made no sense to his rational mind, but which made perfect sense in his chest. In this way he babbled, his head bowed. The chanting and the drums faded to a dull throb.

He cocked his elbow out to the side, changing the angle of the gun's barrel. *The temple? Or further back, maybe above the ear?*

Even as he thought of not existing, the water around him gurgled and came to life, his prayer cut off because he was breathing water. The force of the rising tide stripped the handgun from his hand and spun it off into the dark waters.

Something large and unidentifiable brushed against him. When he opened his eyes, he found his vision clouded by blood…the blood of… He couldn't say.

He didn't float in this world. Down he went, pulled by a force other than gravity. Something wanted him, something needed him to journey into the crimson depths. The red water closed in on him, pressed against his skin hard, until he thought he would burst like a bratwurst left too long on a grill. In his mind, he could feel a seam opening at his navel, the weak spot of his body; it would spread and spread until his body couldn't handle it any longer. Then he would burst, his vital organs ejected into the water where whatever wanted him would feed upon his entrails and the remains of the children he had gifted to the world.

Down he went, spiraling around in the darkness, the pressure in his head building to the point where he tried to figure out which would split first, his belly or his skull.

Stars swam before his eyes, and no longer could he hold his breath. He opened his mouth and let the water in. It was cold, but fresh, salted with blood. The thought crossed his mind to drink his way out of the situation, gulping down infinity until he stood on whatever the bare floor of this place was. His mind, oxygen-starved, stopped thinking rationally.

Then he coughed and sputtered, because he couldn't breathe water. His hands went to his throat, as if he could physically pull the water from his lungs. Bubbles escaped his mouth, kissing his forehead and eyelids as they fluttered upward toward the surface.

One-Shot struck out for the surface, trying to propel himself upward. But his flailing arms and legs had no effect. His descent continued as he coughed and gagged.

Down and down, he sank into the depths.

## Chapter 8: What is Below is Old

One-Shot realized he must have died some time ago. How else could he still be thinking? How else could he still exist under the water despite his inability to breathe? He had been sinking for what seemed like days. His body had stopped trying to breathe altogether. Every time he tried, not because he needed to, but out of habit, he was met with more sputtering, more choking, and more bubbles.

In the blackness of his descent, he relived the errors of his life, viewing it through the filter of his own fracturing mind, trying to pick out which regrets he had caused and which had been foisted upon him. The abortion…that was on him. No, it wasn't. Yes, it was. *You lie to yourself. If you had been normal, Sadie would have kept the kid. If you hadn't been riding the razor's edge of sanity and dulling that edge with booze, she would have kept it.*

*The babies…that's on me. No, it's not. Yes, it is. I wanted money, I wanted to prove to myself I could be a father in the most minimal way possible, and I did, and in the end, with this minimal involvement, I still failed them. They're all dead now because of me, the children I didn't know, the babies I gave nothing but my genetic code and my cursed blood… they are chum now.*

One-Shot drifted further and further away from the world he knew. The sea around him wasn't water, but regret. It wasn't a river or an ocean, but the wound of One-Shot's soul that he'd denied for so long.

In the depths, a light blossomed—faint at first, far away, a light-year or so. One-Shot, accustomed to the pitch-black of the depths, squinted against the glare.

The light dimmed for a second, plunging him into a different form of blindness. It flared once more, and he realized the luminosity wasn't fading, but being blocked by shapes in the water. Flailing dark shapes, spun in circles, their hands at their throats as they kicked their legs, their eyes bugging out of their faces. Among the spasming nightmares, naked and pale, One-Shot sank downward, the light intensifying the closer he came to the source.

One of the shapes drifted by him, near enough for One-Shot to make out his face. A raw wound, like the hole made by a bullet, marred the blue man's forehead. The contents of his skull dribbled out the back of his head as a dark cloud, trailing along behind him like a jellyfish. The man, naked, his eyes horrified, blood-veined and bulging from his eye sockets, seemed to plead with One-Shot for help. One-Shot sailed past him and onto the next monstrosity.

The subsequent wreck twirled through the blackness with limbs broken and rubbery, her belly swollen and ripped open. The edges of the wound flapped with the current like the wings of a manta ray, and her intestines spooled out like the line from a boat's anchor. She spun helplessly, coughing as red bubbles escaped her throat.

*What are they? More chum? More victims of my tribe?*

Everywhere he looked, bits of flesh floated, like one of those Shark Week documentaries. Small bits of humanity bobbed and floated among the current while the maimed, destroyed, and damned swirled about the water like bits of hair circling a drain.

Lower he went, the bodies clogging his descent until he was forced to push the unfortunate souls out of the way, their touch somehow colder than the icy water.

Women, men, children, and the elderly all floated by, their faces conveying their hopelessness. One woman, the hair peeled from her scalp and trailing after her like a shark's fin, opened her mouth to plead with him, red bubbles escaping her throat. But there was nothing he could do.

At any moment, he expected something large and mean to swoop out of the shadows and scoop them up in massive jaws.

Lower and lower he went, and with each foot descended, the corpses and bodies of the living dead appeared in worse condition. A few charred heads floated along, their eyelids blinking in the gloom.

*Where did they come from? How are they still alive?*

Just when he thought he could sink no further, he broke through the red light and into a zone of brilliant white luminescence. Glancing upward, he realized the light hadn't changed; he had simply made it through the bloody, body-filled water.

Below, something massive shifted. This minimal movement still managed to displace a continent's worth of water, and One-Shot found himself buffeted and spun in the wake. When the shockwave had passed and he was done spinning in circles, tumbling end over end, he threw up, his delicious burger and his off-brand french fries spewing out around his face. He breathed in once more and began choking again. It seemed it had been a year since he'd even attempted a breath.

One-Shot jealously watched the bubbles from his lungs ascend upward. When the water cleared once more, the sight of something colossal filled his eyes. Below him, it lurched. Light, painful and burning, singed every inch of his skin until he wanted to turn away. But he couldn't. The sight was too great to ignore.

Below lay a world composed of interlocking plates, each as long as a car. From between those plates, the light emanated, bending around the meshed edges. The scale of the monstrosity below played tricks on his perception, its size so great, he imagined he must be near enough to touch it. When One-Shot held his hand in front of his eyes, he realized how far he had to go. He tumbled further and further. The cold water squeezed the urine and shit out of him, and he closed his eyes against the pressure of the water for fear that his eyeballs would implode in their sockets. In between anguished cries of pain and bouts of choking on the depths, One-Shot squinted through his eyelids periodically to check his progress.

The world shifted around One-Shot, causing the water to brutalize him. When he opened his eyes, he caught a bit of movement to the right. Something massive had shifted there, something so large One-Shot could barely make sense of it.

*This must be what an ant feels like in a human hand. Is this hell?*

With the bright light filtering through his sealed eyelids, his eyes closed, he tried to remember when he had died. Perhaps it was a long time ago—on the highway. Maybe he'd fallen asleep, veered into oncoming traffic, and lay dying on the side of the road right now, his expiring thoughts playing out as an entire lifetime in miniature. Perhaps he'd choked to death at the roadhouse, took too big a bite of delicious hamburger, and suffocated right there and then while everyone looked on. Maybe he'd died in the field with the Whistle Man, traded his own soul for the that of the slain soldier. Now the Whistle Man paraded around Siletz in his skin.

A grumbling, deep-sea purr made blood leak from One-Shot's ears, forced him to open his eyes a crack. What he beheld made him scream. Bubbles of dead air escaped his lungs, obscuring the nightmare before him.

The vastness of the sight made his head swim. He thought he heard a crack as his skull bowed under the pressure. Movement below showered him in a blizzard of bubbles. One-Shot squeezed his eyes shut once more as he thumped into the silt of wherever this place was. He remained on his knees, the weight of the water surging against him, receding, and then crushing him once more.

Another grumble, and suddenly, it hit him. The water had no current. It was being displaced by the breathing of the creature in the depths, the being with the hellish eyes, its body emanating the light of death. He didn't know what to do, how to escape, so he stayed seated, positive he was dead and this was his hell.

*Does time even work here? How long will the tribe wait for me to surface, or did they walk away as soon as I plunged into the water?*

The light on the other side of his eyelids intensified, grew greater, and began to sting his skin like acid. One-Shot leaned forward, digging his hands into the soil before he was blown away, spinning into watery eternity. When the buffeting force stopped, he opened his eyes once more. A face, five-stories-high, vaguely reptilian, gazed at him. The orbs of its eyes glowed, and within their many depths, he could see the history of his people, the suffering and the death. Though he wanted to tear his eyes away, both to relieve the physical pressure of the water and the pressure of watching the deaths of thousands, he couldn't avert his gaze. Few could when gazing upon a god.

His skull cracked once more, pain lancing through his brain. Blood poured from his nose, drifting away in a dark cloud the color of iodine. When he didn't think he could stand the vision any longer, the creature's mouth opened wide. He had expected to find teeth, thousands of them, but instead, a thin membrane stretched like taffy, small breaks in the rubbery surface filtering water through its mouth.

The creature didn't move toward him. It didn't need to. It breathed in, pulling One-Shot from his spot on the ground. He flew through the air in a gritty mess, his arms pinwheeling, blood pouring from his ears and nose. One-Shot slammed into the membrane veiling the monstrosity's mouth. The rubbery material sent him cartwheeling, and his body managed to slip through one of the man-sized openings.

Then the mouth closed, and he was gone.

## Chapter 9: Guts of a God

One-Shot awakened to the soft sound of a drumbeat with the worst hangover of his life. When he opened his eyes, the world glowed an electric white, and black spots swam in front of him. *Was any of it real?*

When he sat up, the bones in his head threatened to come apart, and more blood ran down his face. *It felt real.*

The world within was cold and humid, a miserable combination, but he no longer floated. His blood spilled down his chin and stained his shirt. He pushed himself off the spongy ground, found that the world was entirely black and the lights dancing in his eyes were figments of his damaged brain.

"I want to go home," he sobbed.

There was no answer, no otherworldly voice waiting to guide him, so he did the only thing he could do. He marched through this soft grave, his hands held out in front of him, trying to find the source of the drumbeat. For all he knew, the drumbeat could be in his mind as well.

*Maybe I'm in a coma. My skull is eggshells, my brain is soup, and I'm bleeding out in the real world.*

Onward he walked, for miles, his body shivering in the frigid conditions. If he wasn't dead now, it wouldn't be long before the cold killed him.

Images of the creature he'd seen flashed in his mind, and he fell to the ground. *It's not real. It can't be. We'd know. The world would fucking know if something like that existed.* Denying his reality, he pushed himself to his feet and struck out once more, his hands held before him.

One-Shot's palms encountered a soft wall, and he pressed against it. Immediately, his palms began to sting, as if the very walls could melt him away. *Digested is the word.* Even after he pulled his hands from the wall, his hands continued burning, and he wiped them on his jeans, over and over until they stopped feeling like they were being dissolved. He peeled his shirt off and wrapped it around his hands, his nipples ice hard in the meat locker world. One-Shot continued onward, tracing along a wall, listening to the drumbeat in the darkness.

He walked like this for what seemed like days.

*No one kills kids. They wouldn't kill kids.*

The drumbeat changed then, pouncing on his thoughts, mocking him as the sound of the drumbeat turned into the lub-dub of a heartbeat. He turned toward the sound. It seemed nearer, closer. A weak light appeared dead ahead. It grew brighter until he could make out something strange in the middle of his spongy tomb.

Before him lay a baby, its severed limbs Frankensteined together with crude, monstrous stitches. Blood and yolk-like pus seeped from the wounds. It cried so sharp and so hard One-Shot wanted to put his hands to his ears, but wary of his burned hands and fractured skull, he suffered through the noise. His stomach did flips at the sight, and he tore his eyes from the baby, its arms and legs waving in the air. His tomb was everywhere black, fading away as if reality were but a mist that disappeared after ten feet. The sound of soft trickling teased his ears. Water rose, collecting in the troughs of soft ground at his feet. The baby cried louder, and all One-Shot could do was stand and stare at the child on the pedestal. *Is it one of mine? Is it the one? The one Sadie had…terminated?*

He studied the child's face, tried to find anything of himself in this child. If it was his, maybe he could save it. He supposed he should try either way.

The sound of the infant's heartbeat grew louder, and One-Shot winced as he picked up the child, hoping the sutures holding its limbs together would stay put. If the damn thing fell apart in his arms, he would go crazy.

One-Shot trembled from the frigid embrace of the water as it continued to rise, black and thick. Then the eyes of the baby snapped open, and One-Shot forgot about the cold water altogether. The baby's eyes were not regular eyes. They were pools of infinity, lit by the white-hot void of nothing. In those eyes, One-Shot lost himself, found the history of his people once more, watched as they first climbed from the river, birthed by the infinite being in which he now resided. He watched as they cultivated the world, paved the way for the coming of the depths.

But then they came, the bastard races, the magic scourers—and the tribe became lost. Before they knew what was happening, their language was destroyed, their ability to commune with the true god severed but for those who held the true blood within. One-Shot had it flowing through his veins, as did his uncle before him.

In his mind, a play began. In Act One, he watched as a man he'd only known from faded photo albums, Uncle Harry, cracked under the pressure of communing with a god, broke down under the communication of a being infinitely more complex than himself. Pick up an ant and talk to it, see if it understands, or see if it starts running in your hand. Uncle Harry ran like an ant, disappeared until his broken body washed up on a riverbank.

In Act Two, Uncle Harry's drunken mother—Grandma to One-Shot—drove into the river that same day to do battle with the depths. One-Shot's blood hissed in his veins. It wasn't his blood. He finally understood it was on loan and could be taken back at any time. Something spoke through the fluid coursing through his veins, but it wasn't clear if the thoughts were his or belonged to the being that birthed his people. The creature had spit them out on the riverbanks like a salmon spawning, and then returned to the ocean once more.

One-Shot's eyes snapped open, beheld the baby in his arms, beheld those hideous, eternity eyes, and he began to pull it apart. It had to be done, the longing, the pain, the regrets were holding him back. Here was something he could care for; unlike the bought babies he'd given the world or the wanted one he'd sacrificed in the name of Sadie's career. In destroying this life, he could give birth to something greater, something that would last.

As he fought the stitches of the baby, the water stopped at One-Shot's crotch, the burning cold freezing his genitals. He gritted his teeth, yanked on an arm, a leg, closed his eyes as he heard the rip of stitches, smelled the tang of blood. The heartbeat stopped, and he dropped the baby's remains into the water, stood listening for the drums.

Faintly they came, from a thousand miles away. All he had to do was wait with his own thoughts, deny his own desires.

He must become one with the tribe, give up all his own needs and wants. The tribe came first. The depths would have it no other way. As he dedicated himself to these thoughts, the drumbeat grew closer, louder. His heart synced up with the beat, and the walls and floor vibrated with the rhythm. The drums. The drums. The drums.

One-Shot leaned back and opened his mouth, giving birth to a language that had been almost entirely forgotten by man. The words that escaped rasped from his throat, and he sang the song that would break the world.

# Epilogue: A Spark

They plucked him from the river an hour after he went in the water. As they dragged him upon the banks of the Siletz River, they remarked upon his misshapen head and the blood that poured from his nose. His eyes fluttered, and they prepared to wrestle him to the ground. But there was no need. He came to them willingly, told of the dreams of the people. He was one of them. Though grown far from the field, he was of their crop, one hundred percent.

When he spoke, he spoke twice: once in the bastard language they could understand, and once in the language of their ancestors. The people fawned over him, knew greatness in his words.

"Teach us!" they shouted.

"All in good time!" he said in English. Then he repeated his words in the language of the depths. The syllables, unuttered for a hundred years, wrapped around the people. Their meanings were the same but different. All—the same word as tribe. Good—the same word as a full belly. Time—the same as death.

He walked among them, and in a raucous procession, the tribe flocked to the fire on the hill, where they danced in never-ending circles. Their souls rejoiced for the return of the language that had been taken from them. The drums played on and on, and they sang the song One-Shot taught them, letting it catch in their breast like a spark in a field of dry grass.

By the end of the night, they were on fire, burning from within.

# Acknowledgments

One-Shot was a weird book for me, and it wouldn't be here without help from a ton of people. The first draft of this was written linearly, then I sent it off to Erin Al-Mehairi for her feedback and editing. She talked me out of more pooping and peeing scenes... But not all of them! She also helped me reimagine the book's structure.

After receiving her edits, I realized the linear nature of the tale robbed the beginning of its weirdness and speed. So, I chopped it up and sprinkled One-Shot's particular brand of madness throughout.

Thanks to my advanced readers who gave me feedback on it as well. Your joy for the story gave me the confidence to go shop it around.

Thanks to Kenneth W. Cain for checking it out and taking a chance on this exceedingly non-traditional horror story. Thanks for seeing the vision I had and helping me batter this thing into shape.

Finally, thanks to my fellow writers who gave me blurbs for this one. Shout out to Brian Bowyer, Matt Blairstone, Shane Hawk, and Carlos E. Rivera. You all rock.

Lastly, thanks to anyone who buys this book!

Keep it weird, y'all.

# THE END?

## Not if you want to dive into more of Crystal Lake Publishing's Tales from the Darkest Depths!

Check out our amazing website and online store or download our latest catalog: https://geni.us/CLPCatalog.

We always have great new projects and content on the website to dive into, as well as a newsletter, behind the scenes options, social media platforms, our own dark fiction shared-world series and our very own webstore. Our webstore even has categories specifically for KU books, non-fiction, anthologies, and of course more novels and novellas.

# AUTHOR BIOGRAPHY

Jacy Morris is an Indigenous horror author (a registered member of the Confederated Tribes of Siletz) and a member of the Horror Writers Association. To date, he has written over twenty novels, including the This Rotten World series, the One Night Stand at the End of the World series, and various other works. He is an avid fan of punk rock and horror movies and tries to work this knowledge into his stories. He lives in Portland, Oregon where he works as an English teacher, a writing coach, and an author.

Readers…

Thank you for reading *One-shot*. We hope you enjoyed this novel. If you have a moment, please review *One-Shot* at the store where you bought it.

Help other readers by telling them why you enjoyed this book. No need to write an in-depth discussion. Even a single sentence will be greatly appreciated. Reviews go a long way to helping a book sell, and is great for an author's career. It'll also help us to continue publishing quality books.

Thank you again for taking the time to journey with Crystal Lake's Torrid Waters.

You will find links to all our social media platforms on our Linktree page: https://linktr.ee/CrystalLakePublishing.

# MISSION STATEMENT

Since its founding in August 2012, Crystal Lake has quickly become one of the world's leading publishers of Dark Fiction and Horror books. In 2023, Crystal Lake officially transitioned into an entertainment company, joining several other divisions, genres, and imprints, including Torrid Waters, Crystal Lake Comics, Crystal Lake Games, Crystal Lake Kids, and many more.

While we strive to present only the highest quality fiction and entertainment, we also endeavour to support authors along their writing journey. We offer our time and experience in non-fiction projects, as well as author mentoring and services, at competitive prices.

With several Bram Stoker Award wins and many other wins and nominations (including the HWA's Specialty Press Award), Crystal Lake Publishing puts integrity, honor, and respect at the forefront of our publishing operations.

We strive for each book and outreach program we spearhead to not only entertain and touch or comment on issues that affect our readers, but also to strengthen and support the Dark Fiction field and its authors.

Not only do we find and publish authors we believe are destined for greatness, but we strive to work with men and women who endeavour to be decent human beings who care more for others than themselves, while still being hard working, driven, and passionate artists and storytellers.

Crystal Lake Publishing is and will always be a beacon of what passion and dedication, combined with overwhelming teamwork and respect, can accomplish. We endeavour to know each and every one of our readers, while building personal relationships with our authors, reviewers, bloggers, podcasters, bookstores, and libraries.

We will be as trustworthy, forthright, and transparent as any business can be, while also keeping most of the headaches away from our authors, since it's our job to solve the problems so they can stay in a creative mind. Which of course also means paying our authors.

We do not just publish books, we present to you worlds within your world, doors within your mind, from talented authors who sacrifice so much for a moment of your time.

There are some amazing small presses out there, and through collaboration and open forums we will continue to support other presses in the goal of helping authors and showing the world what quality small presses are capable of accomplishing. No one wins when a small press goes down, so we will always be there to support hardworking, legitimate presses and their authors. We don't see Crystal Lake as the best press out there, but we will always strive to be the best, strive to be the most interactive and grateful, and even blessed press around. No matter what happens over time, we will also take our mission very seriously while appreciating where we are and enjoying the journey.

What do we offer our authors that they can't do for themselves through self-publishing?

We are big supporters of self-publishing (especially hybrid publishing), if done with care, patience, and planning. However, not every author has the time or inclination to do market research, advertise, and set up book launch strategies. Although a lot of authors are successful in doing it all, strong small presses will always be there for the authors who just want to do what they do best: write.

What we offer is experience, industry knowledge, contacts and trust built up over years. And due to our strong brand and trusting fanbase, every Crystal Lake Publishing book comes with weight of respect. In time our fans begin to trust our judgment and will try a new author purely based on our support of said author.

With each launch we strive to fine-tune our approach, learn from our mistakes, and increase our reach. We continue to assure our authors that we're here for them and that we'll carry the weight of the launch and dealing with third parties while they focus on their strengths—be it writing, interviews, blogs, signings, etc.

We also offer several mentoring packages to authors that include knowledge and skills they can use in both traditional and self-publishing endeavours.

We look forward to launching many new careers.

This is what we believe in. What we stand for. This will be our legacy.

Welcome to Crystal Lake Publishing—Where Stories Come Alive!

# Also from Torrid Waters...

In C.L. Kelley's debut novel Corpus, the city's night transforms into a realm of terror.

Nameless, powerful beings, lost in their hunger and forgotten pasts, roam the streets after sunset. But an awakening stirs within them, sharpening their minds and unearthing memories of a dark history and an even darker future.

This chilling foray into vampire fiction pits the hunter against the hunted in a world brimming with supernatural horror and action. Kelley masterfully intertwines multiple perspectives, each character endowed with unique psychic abilities. At the heart of this narrative is a complex villain protagonist, blurring the lines between hero and villain.

The plot thickens with the presence of shapeshifters, adding layers of unpredictability to the already tense atmosphere. Even the seasoned monster hunters find themselves outmatched by these evolving adversaries. The once comforting break of dawn no longer signifies safety.

C.L. Kelley's Corpus is a thrilling exploration of a world where night creatures are not just real but are becoming something more formidable. It's a tale of survival, where the emergence of the dawn might not end the nightmare.

This novel promises an immersive experience into a spine-tingling universe, where every turn of the page brings you closer to the heart of darkness.

# Also from Torrid Waters...

## A fast-paced story of survival,
## terror, family, and friendship.

The people of Wicker thought the mountain belonged to them—purchased with blood, sweat, and resilience. They forgot the deal their ancestors made. They forgot that their mountain belonged to something ancient, powerful, and hungry.

Charlotte Crowe and Rebecca Greenleigh grew up as best friends on the mountain, descendants of the original settlers of Wicker and inheritors of a terrible secret. They expected to grow old on their mountain. They did not expect the return of the wolves, the bone chimes appearing overnight in the trees, or their neighbors turning on one another. In a matter of days, everything they thought they knew is flipped upside down and they find themselves trapped in a place they once called home playing a dangerous game with a creature older than the mountain itself.

# Also from Torrid Waters...

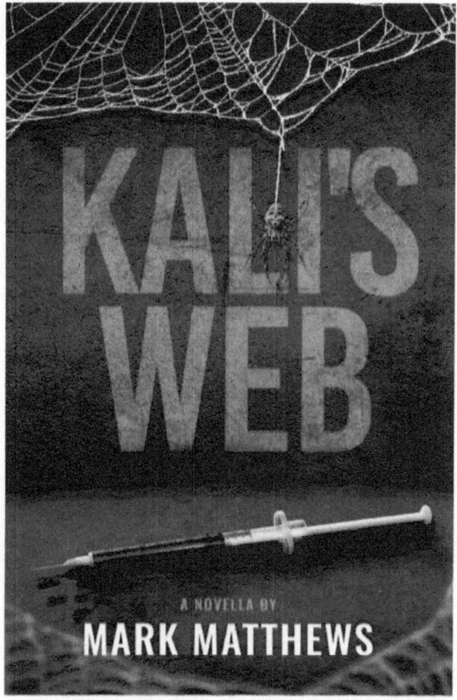

## A tale as dark and complex as the human psyche.

The Kaliana Cook, a heroin addict haunted by her past, is on a desperate quest for freedom. Paroled but longing to reunite with the child she loves, Kali makes a daring escape, only to realize she's entangled in a far more sinister web.

As Kali's journey unfolds, reality warps into a nightmare. She finds herself pursued not only by a relentless parole agent but also by a monstrous presence she unwittingly unleashed. This chilling entity, a bizarre blend of nightmare spiders and a deceptively innocent little girl, embodies the horrors of addiction and the grotesque distortions of a mind plagued by heroin.

Blood and carnage trail Kali's frantic steps, painting a surreal landscape reminiscent of a Cronenbergian nightmare. Her world becomes an unsettling fusion of Trainspotting's raw desperation and the tragic depth of Les Misérables, all shrouded in the eerie innocence of Charlotte's Web. Each moment on the run intensifies Kali's struggle, as she battles not just for her freedom, but for her sanity.

Caught in this twisted web of her own making, Kali faces a harrowing truth: escape is not just about outrunning her physical pursuers, but confronting the haunting specters of her addiction and the supernatural horrors that they manifest.

Kali's Web is a gripping journey into the heart of darkness, exploring the depths of addiction, the potency of the supernatural, and the enduring strength of the human spirit.

Will Kali find her way out of the web, or will you, the reader, be caught in the gripping terror of her journey?

# THANK YOU FOR PURCHASING THIS BOOK